THE
MILLS & BOON®
Centenary Collection

Celebrating 100 years of romance with the very best of Mills & Boon

D1224758

First published in Great Britain 2008
by Harlequin Mills & Boon Limited,
Eton House, 18-24 Paradise Road, Richmond, Surrey TW9 1SR

ISBN: 978 0 263 86646 9

76-1108

Harlequin Mills & Boon policy is to use papers that are
natural, renewable and recyclable products and made from
wood grown in sustainable forests. The logging and
manufacturing processes conform to the legal environmental
regulations of the country of origin.

Printed and bound in Spain
by Litografia Rosés S.A., Barcelona

The Virtuous Widow

by
Anne Gracie

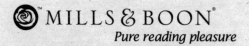

MILLS & BOON

Pure reading pleasure

Anne Gracie was born in Australia, but spent her childhood on the move, living in different parts of Australia, Scotland, Malaysia and Greece. Her days, when not in school, were spent outside with animals and her evenings with her nose in a book – they didn't have TV. She writes in a small room lined with books surrounded by teetering piles of paper. Her first book, *Gallant Waif*, was a RITA® Award finalist for best first book. Anne lives in Melbourne. She has a website, www.annegracie.com, and loves to hear from readers.

Chapter One

⚮

Northumberland, England, December, 1816

"Is my wishing candle still burning, Mama?"

Ellie kissed her small daughter tenderly. "Yes, darling. It hasn't gone out. Now, stop your worrying and go to sleep. The candle is downstairs in the window where you put it."

"Shining out into the darkness so Papa will see it and know where we are."

Ellie hesitated. Her voice was husky as she replied, "Yes, my darling. Papa will know that we are here, safe and warm."

Amy snuggled down under the threadbare blankets and the faded patchwork quilt that covered them. "And in the morning he will be with us for breakfast."

A lump caught in Ellie's throat. "No, darling. Papa will not be there. You *know* that."

Amy frowned. "But tomorrow is my birthday and you said Papa would come."

Tears blurred her eyes as Ellie passed a gentle work-worn hand over her daughter's soft cheek. "No, darling, that was last year. And you know why Papa did not come then."

There was a long silence. "Because I didn't put a candle in the window last year?"

Ellie was horrified. "Oh, no! No, my darling, it had nothing to do with you, I promise you." She gathered the little girl into her arms and hugged her for a long moment, stroking the child's glossy curls, waiting until the lump had gone from her throat and she could speak again. "Darling, your papa died, that's why he never came home."

"Because he couldn't see the way, because I didn't put a candle out for him."

The misery in her daughter's voice pierced Ellie's heart to the core. "No, sweetheart, It wasn't the candle. Papa's death was nobody's fault." It wasn't true. Hart's death had been by his own hand, but gambling and suicide was too ugly a tale for a child.

"Now stop this at once," said Ellie as firmly as she could. "Tomorrow is your birthday and you will be a big girl of four. And do you know what? Because you've been such a good girl and such a help to Mama, there will be a lovely surprise waiting for you in the morning. But only if you go to sleep immediately."

"A surprise? What surprise?" asked the little girl eagerly.

"It wouldn't be a surprise if I told you. Now go to sleep." She began to hum a lullaby, to soothe the anxieties from her daughter's mind.

"I know what the surprise is," murmured her daughter sleepily. "Papa will be here for breakfast."

Ellie sighed. "No, Amy, he won't. Papa has been dead for more than a year. You know he is, so why do you persist with this?"

"It's a special candle, Mama. The lady said so. A wishing candle. It will bring Papa, you'll see." She smiled and snuggled down under the bedclothes, curling up like a little cat.

Ellie frowned. That wretched gypsy woman with her false tales! Unbeknown to her mother, Amy had traded half a dozen eggs and some milk for a thick red candle. A wishing candle, indeed! More like a rather expensive Christmas candle. And a hurtful candle, if the old woman had put the notion in Amy's head that it could bring her father back.

Amy's few memories of her father were idealised fairy tales. The truth was too painful for a little girl. Hart had never been an attentive father or husband. Sir Hartley Carmichael, Baronet, had wanted a son—an heir. A small, spirited girl with tumbled dark curls and bright blue eyes held no interest for him. Was quite useless, in fact, and he'd said so on many occasions—in front of Amy herself.

Ellie looked at her sleeping daughter and her heart filled. There was nothing more precious in the world than this child of hers. She picked up the candle and went into her own room. Shivering in the bitter December cold, she hurriedly slipped into her thick, flannel nightgown and climbed into bed.

She was about to blow the candle out when she recalled the one burning in the downstairs window. Candles were expensive. She couldn't afford to let one burn down to a stub for no purpose. No practical purpose, that is. She recalled her daughter's face, freshly washed for bed and luminous with hope as she placed the candle in the window. A lump filled Ellie's throat. She got out of bed, slipped her shoes back on and flung a shawl around her for warmth. She could not afford the happy dreams that came so easily to children.

She was halfway down the steep, narrow staircase, when suddenly a loud thump rattled the door of her cottage. She froze and waited. Bitter cold crept around her, insidious drafts of freezing air nibbling at her bare legs. She scarcely noticed.

The thump came again. It sounded like a fist hitting the door. Ellie did not move. She hardly dared to breathe. There was a swirl of air behind her and a small, frightened voice behind her whispered, "Is it the squire?"

"No, darling, it isn't. Go back to bed," said Ellie in a low, calm voice.

A small warm paw slipped into her hand, gripping it tightly. "Your hand's cold, Mama." The thump came again, twice this time. Ellie felt her daughter jump in fright.

"It *is* the squire," Amy whispered.

"No, it's not," Ellie said firmly. "He always shouts when I don't open the door to him. Doesn't he?" She felt her daughter's tight grip on her hand relax slightly as the truth of her words sank in. "Wait here, darling, and I shall see who it is."

She crept down another six steps, to where she could see the front door, the sturdy wooden bar she'd put across it looking reassuringly strong. Ellie had soon learned that the cottage keys counted for little against her landlord.

Light flickered and danced intermittently across the dark room from Amy's wishing candle.

Someone banged again, not as loud as before. A deep voice called, "Help!"

"It must be Papa," squeaked Amy suddenly, from close behind her. "He's seen my candle and he's come at last." She slipped past Ellie and raced towards the door.

"No, Amy. Wait!" Ellie followed her, almost falling down the stairs in her rush to prevent her daughter from letting in who-knew-what.

"But it's Papa, Mama. It's Papa," said Amy, trying to lift the heavy bar.

"Hush!" Ellie snatched her daughter to her. "It isn't Papa, Amy. Papa is dead."

Their cottage was isolated, situated a little off the main road and hidden behind a birch spinney. But further along the road was the Angel, an isolated inn which attracted the most disreputable customers. Ellie had twice been followed home… With that den of villains down the road, there was no way she would open her door to a stranger at night.

The deep voice called again, "Help." It sounded weaker this time. He hit the door a couple of times, almost half-heartedly. Or as if he was running out of strength, Ellie thought suddenly. She bit her lip, holding her daughter against her. It might be a ruse to trick her.

"Who is it?" she called. There was no reply, just the sound of something falling. Then silence. Ellie waited for a moment, hopping from one foot to the other in indecision. Then she made up her mind. "Stand on the stairs, darling," she ordered Amy. "If it's a bad man, run to your room and put the bar across your door, as I showed you—understand?"

Amy nodded, her heart-shaped little face pale and

frightened. Ellie picked up the heaviest pan she had. She turned the key and lifted the bar. Raising the pan, she took a deep breath and flung open the door.

A flurry of sleet blew in, causing her to shiver. She peered out into the darkness. Nobody. Not a sound. Still holding the pan high, she took a tentative step forward to look properly and encountered something large and cold huddled on her doorstep.

It was a man, lying very, very, still. She bent and touched his face. Cold. Insensible. Her fingers touched something wet, warm and sticky. Blood. He was bleeding from the head. There was life still in him, but not if she left him outside in the freezing weather for much longer. Dropping the pan she grabbed him by the shoulders and tugged. He was very heavy.

"Is he dead, Mama?" Amy had crept back down the stairs.

"No, darling, but he's hurt. We need to bring him inside to get warm. Run and fetch the rug from in front of the fire, there's a good girl."

Amy scampered off and returned in a moment dragging the square, threadbare cloth. Ellie placed it as close as she could to the man's prone body, then pushed and pushed until finally he rolled over onto the rug. Then she pulled with all her might. Amy pulled too. Inch by inch the man slid into the cottage. Ellie subsided on the floor, gasping.

She barred the door again and lit a lantern. Their unexpected guest wore no jacket or coat—only a shirt and breeches. And no shoes, just a pair of filthy, muddied stockings. And yet it was December, and outside there was sleet and ice.

Blood flowed copiously from a nasty gash at the back

of his head. Hit from behind; a cowardly blow. He'd been stripped of his belongings, even his coat and boots, and left to die in the bitter cold. Ellie knew what it felt like to lose everything. She laid a hand on his chest, suddenly possessive. She could not help his being robbed, but she would *not* let him die.

His shirt was sopping wet and freezing to the touch, the flesh beneath it ominously cold. Quickly she made a pad of clean cloth and bound it around his forehead as tight as she dared to staunch the blood.

"We'll have to get these wet clothes off him," she told Amy. "Else he'll catch his death of cold. Can you bring me some more towels from the cupboard under the stairs?" The child ran off as Ellie stripped the man's shirt, undershirt and wet, filthy stockings off.

He had been severely beaten. His flesh was abraded and beginning to show bruises. There were several livid, dark red, curved marks as if he'd been kicked and one clear imprint of a boot heel on his right shoulder. She felt his ribs carefully and gave a prayer of thanks that they seemed to have been spared. His head injury was the worst, she thought. He would live, she thought, as long as he didn't catch a chill and sicken of the cold.

Carefully, she rubbed a rough-textured towel over the broad planes of his chest and stomach and down his arms. Her mouth dried. She had only ever seen one man's naked torso before. But this man was not like her husband.

Hart's chest had been narrow and bony, white and hairless, his stomach soft, his arms pale, smooth and elegant. This man's chest was broad and hard, but not bony. Thick bands of muscles lay relaxed now in his un-conscious state, but firm and solid, nevertheless. A light dusting of soft, curly dark hair formed a wedge over the golden skin, arrowing into a faint line of hair trailing down his stomach and disappearing into his breeches. She tried not to notice it as she scrubbed him with the towel, forcing warmth and life back into his chilled skin.

He was surprisingly clean, she thought. His flesh did not have that sour odour she associated with Hart's flesh. This man smelt of nothing—perhaps a faint smell of soap, and of fresh sweat and…was it leather? Horses? Whatever it was, Ellie decided, it was no hardship to be so close to him.

Despite his muscles, he was thin. She could count each of his ribs. And his stomach above the waistband of his breeches was flat, even slightly concave. His skin carried numerous small scars, not recent injuries. A man who had spent his life fighting, perhaps. She glanced at his hands. They were not the soft white hands of a gentleman. They were strong and brown and battered, the knuckles skinned and swollen. He was probably a farm labourer or something like that. That would explain his muscles and his thinness. He was not a rich man, that was certain. His clothes, though once of good quality, were old and well worn. The shirt had been inexpertly patched a number of times. As had his breeches.

His breeches. They clung cold and sodden to his form. They would have to come off. She swallowed as she reached for his waistband, then hesitated, as her daughter arrived with a bundle of towels. "Good girl. Now run upstairs, my love, and fetch me a blanket from my bed and also the warm brick that's in it."

Amy trotted off and Ellie took a deep breath. She was not unacquainted with the male form, she told herself firmly, as she unbuttoned the stranger's drenched breeches. She had been married. But this man was not her husband. He was much bigger, for a start.

She grasped the breeches and tugged them over his hips, rolling him from side to side as she worked them downwards. The heavy wet fabric clung stubbornly to his chilled flesh. Finally she had them off him. Panting, she sat back on her heels. He was naked. She stared, unable to look away.

"Is Papa all right?" Amy came down the stairs, carefully lugging a bundled-up blanket.

Hastily, Ellie tucked a towel over the stranger's groin. "He's *not* your papa."

Amy gave her an odd look, then raced back upstairs. Ellie dragged the man as close as she could to the fire. When Amy returned with the brick, Ellie placed it in the hearth. She heated some soup, then strained it through a piece of muslin into the teapot.

"Soup in the *teapot?*" Amy giggled at something so silly.

Ellie smiled, relieved that her daughter found something to laugh at. "This is going to take some time, so it's back to bed for you, young lady."

"Oh, but, Mama—"

"The man will still be here in the morning," Ellie said firmly. "We already have one sick person here—I don't want you to catch a chill as well. So, miss, off to bed at once." She kissed her daughter and pushed her gently towards the door. Reluctantly, Amy went. Ellie hid a smile. Her curious little puss would stay up all night if she could.

She cleaned his head wound thoroughly, then laid a pad of hot, steaming herbs on it, to draw out any remaining impurities. He groaned and tried to move his head.

"Hush." She smoothed a hand over his skin, keeping the hot poultice steady with her hand. "It stings a little, but it's doing you good." He subsided, but Ellie felt tension in his body as if part of him was awake. Defensive. She soothed him gently, murmuring, "Rest quietly. Nobody will harm you here." Slowly his big body relaxed.

His eyelids flickered, then his eyes slowly opened. Ellie bent over him earnestly, still supporting his head in her hand. "How do you feel?" she asked softly.

The stranger said nothing, just stared at her out of blue, blue eyes.

How did he feel? Like his head was about to split open. He blinked at her, trying to focus on her face. Pretty face, he thought vaguely. Soft, smooth skin. His eyes followed the fall of shining dark hair from her smooth creamy brow, down to a tumble of soft curls around her shoulders.

Who was she? And where the devil were they? With an effort he glanced away from her for a second, taking in the room. Small…a cottage? Had he been billeted in some nearby cottage? They did that sometimes with the wounded. Left them to the dubious care of some peasant woman while the fighting moved on… He frowned, trying to recall. Had they won the battle or lost it? Or was it still raging? He listened. No, there was no sound of guns.

His gaze returned to the woman. The cottage told him nothing. But the woman… He couldn't take his eyes off her. Soft, worried eyes. Soft worried mouth. Pretty mouth. Worried? Or frightened? He had no idea.

He tried to move and heard himself groan. His head was killing him. Like someone had taken an axe to it. How had that happened? Was he bleeding? He tried to feel his head. And found he could not move. Trapped, dammit! He could not move his hands and legs. Someone had tied him up. He'd been taken prisoner. He began to struggle.

"Hush," the woman said soothingly. She began to loosen the bindings around his arms as she spoke. "It's all right. I just wrapped you tight in my blanket because you were all wet and I feared you would take a chill."

He blinked up at her. His head throbbed unbearably. The rest of his body ached as well, but his head was the worst. Dizziness and confusion washed over him.

And then it hit him. She had spoken in English. Not Portuguese, or Spanish or French. English—not foreigners' English, either—proper English. His sort of English. So where were they? He tried to speak, to ask her. He felt his mouth move, but it was as if someone had cut out his tongue. Or severed it from his brain. He felt his lips moving, but no words came out. He fixed his gaze on her face and tried to muster the energy to ask her the question. Questions. They crowded his splitting head.

The woman sat down on the floor beside him again and smoothed his hair gently back from his forehead. It felt so good, he closed his eyes for a moment to savour it.

"I don't have any brandy," she said apologetically. "All I have is hot soup. Now, drink a little. It will give you strength and warmth."

Warmth? Did he need warmth? He realised that he was shivering. She lifted his head up and though he knew she was being as gentle as she could be, his brain thundered and swirled and he felt consciousness slipping from him. But then she tucked him against her shoulder and held him there, still and secure and somehow…cared for. He gripped her thigh and clung stubbornly to his senses and gradually felt the black swirling subside.

He recoiled as something clunked against his teeth. "It is only the teapot," she murmured in his ear. "It contains warm broth. Now, drink. It will help."

He wanted to tell her that he was a man, that he would drink it himself, out of a cup, not a teapot, like some helpless infant, but the words would not come. She tipped the teapot up and he had to swallow or have it spill down him. He swallowed. It was good broth. Warm. Tasty. It warmed his insides. And she felt so soft and good, her breasts against him, her arm around him, holding him upright against her. Weakly, he closed his eyes and allowed himself to be fed like a baby.

He drank the broth slowly, in small mouthfuls. The woman's breath was warm against his face. She seemed to know how much to give him and when he needed to wait between mouthfuls. He could smell her hair. He wanted to turn his head and bury his face in it. He drank the broth instead. The fire crackled in the grate. Outside the wind whistled and howled, rattling at the doors and windows. It was chilly inside the cottage, and the floor underneath him was hard and cold, but oddly, he felt warm and cosy and at peace.

He finished the broth and half-sat, half-lay against her, allowing her to wipe his mouth, like a child. They sat for a moment or two, in companionable silence, with the wind swirling outside the cottage and the questions swirling inside his head.

Beneath the blanket he was stark naked, he suddenly realised. He stared at her, another question on his unmoving lips. Who was she, to strip him of his clothes?

As if she knew what he wanted, she murmured gently in his ear, "You arrived at my cottage almost an hour ago.

I don't know what happened to you before that. You were half-dressed and sopping wet. Frozen from the sleet and the rain. I don't know how long you'd been outside, or how you managed to find the cottage, but you collapsed at the door—"

"Is Papa awake now?" a little voice said, like the piping of a bird.

Papa? He opened his eyes and saw a vivid little face staring at him with bright, inquisitive eyes. A child. A little girl.

"Go back to bed this instant, Amy," said the woman sharply.

He winced and jerked his head and the blackness swirled again. When he reopened his eyes, he wasn't sure how much time had passed. He was no longer leaning against the woman's shoulder and the little face of the child was gone. And he was shivering. Hard.

The woman bent over him, her eyes dark with worry. "I'm sorry," she murmured. "I didn't mean to bump you like that. My daughter gave me a fright, that was all. Are you all right?" A faint frown crumpled the smoothness of her brow. "The bleeding has stopped and I have bandaged your head."

He barely took in her words. All he could think of was that his head hurt like the devil and she was worried. He lifted a hand and stroked down her cheek slowly with the back of his fingers. It was like touching fine, cool, soft satin.

She sighed. And then she pulled back. "I'm afraid you will freeze if I leave you down here on the stone floor. Even with the fire going all night—and I don't have the fuel for that— the stone floor will draw all the warmth from your body."

He could only stare at her and try to control the shivering.

"The only place to keep you warm is in bed." She blushed and did not meet his eye. "There…there is only one bed."

He frowned, trying to absorb what she was telling him, but unable to understand why it would distress her. He still couldn't recall who she was—the blow had knocked all sense from his head—but the child had called him 'Papa.' He tried to think, but the effort only made the pain worse.

"It is upstairs. The bed. I cannot carry you up there."

His confusion cleared. She was worried about his ability to get up the stairs. He nodded and gritted his teeth over the subsequent waves of swirling blackness. He could do that much for her. He would climb her stairs. He did not like to see her worried. He held out his hand to her and braced himself to stand. He wished he could remember her name.

Ellie took his arm and heaved until he was upright—shaky and looking appallingly pale, but standing and still conscious. She tucked the blanket tight under his armpits and knotted it over his shoulder, like a toga. She hoped it was warm enough. His feet and his long brawny calves were bare and probably cold, but it was better than having him trip. Or naked.

She wedged her shoulder under his armpit and steered him towards the stairs. The first step was in a narrow doorway with a very low lintel, for the cottage had not been designed for such tall men as he.

"Bend your head," she told him. Obediently, he bent, but lost his balance and lurched forward. Ellie clung to him, pulling him back against the doorway, to keep him upright.

Fearful that he would straighten and hit his injury on the low beam, she cupped one hand protectively around his head and drew it down against her own forehead for safety. He leaned on her, half-unconscious, breathing heavily, one arm around her, one hand clutching the wooden stair-rail, his face against hers. White lines of pain bracketed his mouth.

There were only fourteen steep and narrow stairs, but it took a superhuman effort to get him up them. He seemed barely conscious, except for the grim frown of concentration on his face and the slow determined putting of one foot in front of the other. He gripped the stair-rail with fists of stone and hauled himself up, pausing at each step achieved, reeling with faintness. Ellie held him tightly, supporting him with all the strength she could muster. He was a big man; if he collapsed, she could not stop him falling. And if he fell, he might never regain consciousness.

There was little conversation between them, only the grim, silent battle. One painful step at a time. From time to time, she would murmur encouragement—"we are past the halfway mark," "only four steps left"—but she had no idea if he understood. The only sound he made was a grunt of exertion, or the raw harsh panting of a man in pain, at the end of his tether. He hung on to consciousness by willpower alone. She had never seen such stubbornness, or such courage.

At last they reached the top of the stairs. Straight ahead of them was the tiny room where Amy's bed was tucked— no more than a narrow cupboard it was, really, but cosy enough and warm for her daughter. On the right was Ellie's bedroom.

"Bend your head again." This time she was ready when he lurched forward and stumbled into her room. She managed to steer him to the small curtained-off alcove where her bed stood. He sprawled across it with a groan and lay there, unmoving. She collapsed beside him, gasping for breath, weak with relief. Her breath clouded visibly in the icy air. She had to get him covered, while he was still warm from the exertion of the climb.

She had no nightshirt for him to wear. He was too broad in the shoulders and chest for any of her clothing and she had long ago sold anything of Hart's that remained. The few thin blankets she had did not look warm enough to keep an unconscious man from catching a chill. The thickest, warmest coverings were on Amy's bed.

She wrapped him in a sheet and tugged the covers over him. She took all the clothes she possessed and spread them out over the bed—dresses, shawls, a faded pelisse, a threadbare cloak—any layer of cloth which would help keep out the cold. She fetched the hot brick and set it at his feet. Then she stood back. She could do no more. She was shivering herself, she realised. And her feet were frozen. She normally got into bed to keep warm.

But tonight there was a strange man in her bed.

Amy's bed was only a narrow bench, as long and as wide as a child. No room for Ellie there. Downstairs, the fire was dying. Ellie sat on the wooden stool, drew her knees against her chest and wrapped her shawl even tighter around herself in an illusion of warmth. She had used up all her extra clothes to make the bed warm for the stranger. She stared across at him. He lay there, warm, relaxed, comfortable while she hugged herself against the cold. He had collapsed. He was insensible. He wouldn't know she was there.

She crept to the edge of the bed on frozen toes and looked at him. He lay on his back, his breathing deep and regular. In the frail light of the candle the bandage glimmered white against his tanned skin and the thick, dark, tousled hair. There was a shadow of dark bristle on his lean, angular jaw. He seemed so big and dark and menacing in her bed. He took up much more of it than she did. And what if he woke?

She couldn't do this. She crept back to her stool. The chill settled. Drafts whispered up at her, insinuating themselves against her skin, nibbling at her like rats. Her chattering teeth echoed a crazed counterpoint to his deep, even breaths.

She had no choice. It was her bed, after all. It would do nobody any good if she froze to death out here. What mattered propriety when it came to her very health? She ran downstairs again and fetched her frying pan. She took a deep breath, wrapped the sheet more tightly around herself and stepped into the sleeping alcove, frying pan in hand. Feeling as if she were burning her bridges, she closed the curtains which kept the cold drafts out. In the tiny, enclosed space, she felt even more alone with the stranger than ever…

Outside, pellets of hail beat against her window.

Carefully, stealthily, Ellie tucked the pan under the edge of the mattress, comfortingly to hand, then crept under the bedclothes. He wasn't just in her bed, he took up most of the space. And almost all of the bedclothes. Without warning, she found herself lying hard against him, full length, his big body touching hers from shoulder to ankle. Threadbare sheets were all that lay between them. Ellie went rigid with anxiety. She poked him. "Hsst!

Are you awake?" Her hand hovered, ready to snatch up the pan.

He didn't move; he just lay there, breathing slowly and evenly as he had for the last fifteen minutes. She tried to move away from him, but his weight had caused the mattress to sag. Her body could not help but roll downhill towards him. Against him. It was a most unsettling sensation. She wriggled a little, trying to reduce the contact between them. Her frozen toes slipped from their sheet and touched his long legs…and she sighed with pleasure. He was warm, like a furnace.

Fever? She put out a hand in the darkness and felt his forehead. It seemed cool enough. But that could be the effect of the cold night air. She slipped a hand under the bedclothes and felt his chest. The skin was warm and dry, the muscles beneath it firm. He didn't feel feverish at all. He felt…nice.

She snatched her hand away and tucked herself back in her own cocoon of bedclothes. She closed her eyes firmly, trying to shut out the awareness of the man in her bed. Of course, she would not get a wink of sleep—she was braced against the possibility that he was awake, shamming unconsciousness, but at least she would be warm.

She had never actually slept with a man before. Hart had not cared to stay with her longer than necessary. After coitus he had immediately left her, and once she had quickened with child he had never returned to her bed. So the very sensation of having a man sleep beside her was most…unsettling.

She could smell him, smell the very masculine smell of his body, the scent of the herbal poultice she had made for his injury. His big, hard body seemed to fill the bed. It lifted the bedclothes so that there was a gap between him and her smaller frame, a gap for cold drafts to creep into. She wriggled closer, to close the gap a little, still lying rigid, apart from him, straining against the dip in the mattress.

Slowly, insidiously, his body heat warmed her and gradually her defences relaxed. The combination of his reassuring stillness and the regularity of his deep breathing eased her anxious mind until finally she slept.

And as she slept, her body curled against his, closing the gap seamlessly. Her cold toes slipped from their cool linen cocoon and rested on the hard warmth of his long bare calves. And her hand crept out and snuggled itself between the layers that wrapped him, until it was resting on that warm, firm, broad masculine chest…

Weak winter sun woke her, lighting the small, spare room, setting a golden glow through the faded curtains that covered her sleeping alcove. Feeling cosy, relaxed and contented, Ellie yawned sleepily and stretched…and found herself snuggled hard against a man's ribs, her feet curled around his leg, her arm across his prone body.

She shot out of bed like a stone from a catapult and stood there shivering in the sudden cold, staring at the stranger, blinking as it all came back to her. She snatched some of her clothes and hurried downstairs to get the fire going again.

The man slept on through the day. Apart from him sleeping like the dead, Ellie could find nothing wrong with him. She checked his head wound several times. It was no longer bleeding and showed no sign of infection. His breathing was deep and even. He wasn't feverish and he didn't toss and turn. He muttered occasionally, and each time, Amy came running to tell.

Amy was fascinated by him. Ellie had managed to stop her daughter referring to the stranger as Papa, but she couldn't seem to keep her away from his bedside. The weather was too bitter for her to play outside and the size of the cottage meant that if Amy wasn't with Ellie downstairs, she was upstairs watching the man.

It was harmless, Ellie told herself. And rather sweet. While Amy played with her dolls upstairs, she told him long, rambling stories and sang him songs, a little off-key. She told him of her special red wishing candle, that had brought him home. The child seemed quite unperturbed that he never responded to her prattle, that he just slept on.

It would be a different story when he woke. If he ever did wake…

She probably should have fetched Dr. Geddes. But she disliked him intensely. Dr. Geddes dressed fashionably, yet his tools of trade were filthy. He would bleed the man, give him a horrid-tasting potion of his own invention and charge a large fee. Ellie had little money and even less faith in him. Besides, Dr. Geddes was a friend of the squire…

She folded the shirt, now clean and dry, and set it with his buckskin breeches on the chest in her room. Both garments had once been of good quality, but had seen hard wear and tear. There was nothing incongruous about a poor labourer wearing such clothes, however. In the last year she had been amazed to learn of the thriving trade in used clothing—second-, third-, even fourth-hand clothing.

Even things she'd thought at the time were total rags she knew now could have been sold for a few pennies, or a farthing.

She'd sold everything too cheaply, she realised in retrospect. Her jewellery, her furniture, treasured possessions, Amy's clothes, her beautiful dolls' house, with its exquisitely made furnishings, the tiny, perfect dolls with their lovely clothes and charming miniature knick-knacks—she could have sold them to far more purpose now. She had been ignorant, then, of the true value of things.

Still, they were neither starving nor frozen, and her daughter derived just as much pleasure from her current dolls' house, made from an old cheese box, with home-made dolls and furnishings made from odds and ends.

Ellie examined the stranger's other belongings. There were precious few—just the clothes he stood up in. His stockings were thick and coarse but walking on the bare ground in them had made holes, which she had yet to darn. She had found no other belongings to give a clue to his identity, only one item found wadded in his breeches pocket, a delicate cambric handkerchief, stiff with dried blood. An incongruous thing for such a man to be carrying. It did not go with the rest of him, his strong hands and his bruised knuckles.

She recalled the way those big, battered knuckles had slipped so gently across her cheek and sighed. Such a small, unthinking gesture…it had unravelled all her resolve to keep him at a distance.

He was a stranger, she told herself sternly. A brawler and possibly a thief as well. She hoped he had not stolen the handkerchief. It was bad enough having a strange man sleeping in her bed, let alone a thief.

Rat-tat-tat! Ellie jumped at the sound.

Amy's eyes were big with fright. "Someone at the door, Mama," she whispered.

"Miz Carmichael?" a thick voice shouted.

"It's all right, darling. It's only Ned. Just wait here." Ellie put aside her mending and went to answer the door. She hesitated, then turned to her daughter. "You mustn't tell Ned, or anyone else, about the man upstairs, all right? It's a secret, darling."

Her daughter gazed at her with solemn blue eyes and nodded. "'Coz of the squire," she said, and went back to playing with her dolls' house.

Ellie closed her eyes in silent anguish, wishing she could have protected her daughter from such grim realities. But there was nothing she could do about it. She opened the door.

"Brought your milk and the curds you wanted, Miz Carmichael," said the man at the door and added, "Thought you might like these 'uns, too." He handed her a brace of hares. "Make a nice stew, they will. No need to tell the squire, eh?" He winked and made to move off.

"Ned, you shouldn't have!" Ellie was horrified, and yet she couldn't help clutching the dead animals to her. It was a long time since she and Amy had eaten any meat, and yet Ned could hang or be transported for poaching. "I wouldn't for the world get you into troub—"

Ned chuckled. "Lord love ye, missus, don't ye worry about me—I bin takin' care o' Squire's extra livestock all me life, and me father and granfer before me."

"But—"

The grizzled man waved a hand dismissively. "A gift for little missie's birthday."

There was nothing Ellie could say. To argue would be

to diminish Ned's gift, and she could never do that. "Then I thank you, Ned. Amy and I will very much enjoy them." She smiled and gestured back into the cottage. "Would you care to come in, then, and have a cup of soup? I have some hot on the fire."

"Oh, no, no, thank ye, missus. I'd not presume." He shuffled his feet awkwardly, touched his forehead and stomped off into the forest before she could say another word.

Ellie watched him go, touched by the man's awkwardness, his pride and the risky, generous gift. The hares hung heavy in her arms. They would be a feast. And the sooner they were in the pot, the safer it would be for all concerned. She had planned to make curd cakes for Amy's birthday surprise. Now they would both enjoy a good, thick meaty stew as well—it would almost be a proper birthday celebration. And if the man upstairs ever woke up, she would have something substantial to feed him, too.

She smiled to herself as she struggled to strip the skin from the first hare. She'd thought him a thief because of the handkerchief. Who was she to point her finger, Ellie Carmichael, proud possessor of two fat illegal hares…?

He had slept like the dead now, for a night and a day. Ellie stared at his shape and wished she could do something. She wanted him awake. She wanted him up and out of her bed. She wanted him gone. It was unsettling, having him there, asleep in her bedclothes. It was not so difficult to get used to it during the day, to assume he was harmless, to allow her daughter to sit beside him, treating an unconscious man—a complete stranger—as if he was one of her playthings. During the day he didn't seem so intimidating. Now…

She hugged her wrapper tighter around her, trying to summon the courage to climb into the bed beside him once more. In the shadows of the night he seemed to grow bigger, darker, more menacing, the virile-looking body sprawled relaxed in her bed more threatening.

But he hadn't stirred for a night and a day. Another night of sharing would do no harm, surely. Besides, she didn't have any choice… No, she'd made a choice, her conscience corrected her. She could have called for help. He would have been taken "on the parish." But he wouldn't have received proper care—not with the poor clothing he wore. An injured gentleman, yes, the doctor or even the squire would see to his care. But there were too many poor and injured men in England since the war against Napoleon had been won. They'd returned as brief heroes. Now, months later, as they searched for work or begged in the streets, they'd come to be regarded as a blight on the land. It wouldn't matter if one more died.

There were too many indigent widows and little girls, too.

She could not abandon him. Somehow, with no exchange of words between them, she had made herself responsible for this man—stranger or not, thief or not. He was helpless and in need. Ellie knew what it felt like to be helpless and in need. And she would help him.

Without further debate, Ellie wrapped herself in her separate sheet—she hadn't lost all sense of propriety— and slipped into the bed beside him. She sighed with pleasure. He was better than a hot brick on a cold winter's night.

This time there was little sense of strangeness. She was used to his masculine smell, she even found it appealing.

The sag of the bed felt right, and she didn't struggle too hard against it. After all, if there was too much of a gap between them, icy drafts would get in. But recalling the immodest position she had woken in, she determinedly turned her back to him. It was not so intimate, having one's back against a stranger, she thought sleepily, as she snuggled her backside against his hip.

And once again, in the warmth of his body heat and the calm steady rhythm of his deep, even breathing, Ellie forgot her fears of the stranger and went to sleep. And her toes reached out and curled contentedly against his calves…

Ellie came awake slowly to a delicious sense of…pleasure. She had been having the most delectable dream. She kept her eyes closed, prolonging the delightful sensation of being…loved. Hart was caressing her in the way she had always dreamed of… His big, warm hands smoothing, kneading, loving her skin. She felt beautiful, loved, desired in a way she had never before felt. Warm, sleepy, smiling, she stretched and moved sensually, squirming pleasurably in the grip of the marvellous dream. Her skin felt alive as his hands moved over, across, around, between…sending delicious shivers through her body, shivers which had nothing to do with the cold and everything to do with…desire.

Hands slipped up her thighs and caressed her hips and she moved restlessly, her legs trembling. She felt a big, warm hand cup one breast, felt her flesh move silkily against the rougher skin of his hand. Her breasts seemed to swell under the caress and when she felt warm breath against her naked skin she clenched her eyes shut and felt her body arch with pleasure. A hot mouth closed over her breast and his tongue rubbed gently back and forth across her turgid nipple. She shuddered uncontrollably, waves of pleasure and excitement juddering through her with a force she had never experienced. He sucked, hard, and she almost came off the bed in shock as hot spears of ecstasy drove though her body. She could barely think, only feel. Her hands gripped his shoulders and gloried in the feel of his power and the smooth, naked skin under her palms.

Still creating those glorious sensations at her breast, she felt a large, calloused hand smooth down over her belly, caressing, smoothing, exciting… Her legs fell apart, trembling with need.

His mouth came down over hers, softly, tenderly, possessively, nipping gently at her lips. "Open," he murmured huskily, and their mouths merged as his tongue tasted her, learned her, possessed her, and she tasted him and learned him in response.

And froze…

It wasn't Hart! Ellie jerked her head back and opened her eyes. *It wasn't Hart!*

He smiled at her early morning bewilderment. "Morning, love."

It was the stranger! It hadn't been a harmless, delicious dream of her husband. She had been lying with a stranger! Allowing him intimacies even her husband had never taken. Her breast still throbbed with want. And his hand was still creating the most incredible sensations between her— With a small scream, Ellie shoved him away from her and shot out of bed. There was a thud as his head connected with a bedpost and he swore. She stood shivering in the middle of the room, staring at him, outraged, dragging her nightgown down over her flushed and trembling nakedness.

"Who are you? How—how dare you! Get out—get out of my bed!"

"You didn't need to shove so hard," he grumbled. "My head was bad enough when I woke. Now it feels like—"

"I don't care what your head feels like! I said, get out!" Ellie almost screeched it.

He blinked at her in puzzlement, rubbing his head absently. "What's the matter, love?"

"As if you don't know, you—you ravisher! Get out of my bed!"

He frowned in vague confusion, then shrugged, climbed out and walked towards her. Stark naked. Acres of naked masculine skin, bared to her shocked gaze. With not a shred of shame.

"Stop! Get back!" She felt her whole body blushing in response.

He gave her a very male look, as if to say, make up your mind, but he stopped his movement towards her and sat back down on the bed, rubbing his head. Still naked. Making no attempt to cover himself. Even though he was still shamefully, powerfully aroused.

As, even more shamefully, was she. Her knees trembled, so she sat on the stool, half-turned away from the beautiful, shocking sight of him. "Cover yourself!" Ellie snapped.

She heard a slither of fabric, and turning back to face him, she felt herself blush again. He had picked up one of her stockings and draped it carefully across himself. Across the part which had most shocked her. The rest of him sat there in shameless naked glory. His body was glorious, too. She tried not to notice how much.

His blue, blue eyes were twinkling roguishly. "Is that better, love?"

"Don't call me that!" she snapped. "And cover yourself properly. My daughter could come in at any moment."

At her words he glanced towards the door and drew one of the blankets around his shoulders, covering his chest and torso and…the rest. It didn't seem to make him any less naked. His long legs, bare, brawny and boldly masculine, were braced apart on the edge of the bed. She tried not to think about what the blanket concealed.

"You'll have to leave," Ellie said firmly. "I shall go downstairs and make you some breakfast while you dress yourself. And then you will have to leave."

He frowned. "Where do you want me to go?"

Ellie stared in astonishment. "Where do *I* want you to go? Go wherever you want. It's nothing to do with me."

"Are you so angry with me, then?" His voice was soft, deep and filled with concern.

Ellie recalled the shocking things he had done to her. It seemed even worse that she had enjoyed them so much. "Of course I am angry. What did you expect when you attacked me in that appalling way?"

His brow furrowed. "Attacked?" His brow cleared after a minute and he looked incredulous. "You mean just now, in bed? But you were enjoying it as much as I was."

Ellie went scarlet. "Oh, you are shameless! I want you out of my house this instant!" As she spoke, his stomach rumbled. "As soon as you have eaten," she amended gruffly, feeling foolish. It was ridiculous to care whether he was hungry or not. She had taken in a stranger and cared for him for several days and how had he repaid her? With near-ravishment, that's how! The scoundrel! She wanted him out!

There was a short silence. "Did we have a quarrel, love?"

"Quarrel!" Ellie said wrathfully. "I'll give you quarrel! And I *told* you not to call me that!"

"Call you what?" He frowned. "Love?"

Ellie flushed and nodded curtly.

He rubbed his head and then said in an embarrassed voice. "I'm sorry if it makes you cross, but the truth is, I have the devil of a head on me and cannot seem to recall your name."

"It is Ellie. Mrs. Ellie Carmichael," she added for emphasis. Better he think she was married, not a widow. He might leave faster if he thought she expected a husband home any minute. It was Lady Carmichael, in truth, but it seemed ludicrous for a pauper to be titled.

"Ellie," he said softly. "I like it…Carmichael, eh?" He frowned, as if suddenly confused. "Then—"

"What you think of my name is immaterial to me." Ellie tossed him his clothes. "Have the goodness to dress yourself at once and leave this house!"

"Why do you want me to leave?"

Ellie narrowed her eyes at him. "Because this is my home and I say who can stay here! And you, sir, have out-stayed your welcome!"

He looked at her seriously. "And have I no rights?"

She gasped at his audacity. "*Rights!* And what rights, pray, do you think you may have here, sirrah!" Did he think a few stolen caresses gave him rights? She was no doxy!

He hesitated, looking oddly uncertain. "Is this property not in my name?"

"*Your* name? Why should it be?" Ellie glared at him, but could not help feeling suddenly frightened at this talk of rights. What if the squire had sold the cottage without telling her? He had threatened to do so, often enough. Nor would she be surprised to learn he would imply that Ellie was part of the sale. The squire was a vindictive man.

"Women do not commonly own property. It is generally held in the husband's name."

The squire *had* sold the cottage. And this man had bought it for his wife and himself. And had been set upon by thieves while on his way to inspect his new property. Fear wrapped itself around Ellie's throat but she drew herself up proudly. "I am not for sale. My daughter and I will leave this place as soon as possible. You will give us a week or two, I presume, out of simple decency."

"Dammit, woman, you don't have to go anywhere!" he roared. "What sort of man do you think I am?"

"I have not the slightest idea," said Ellie frostily. "Nor do I care. But I am *not* for sale!"

"Who the devil suggested you were, for heaven's sake!" he said, exasperated, and clutched his head again. "Blast this head of mine. What the deuce is the matter with it?"

"Someone hit you," said Ellie. He gave her a look, which she ignored. "I do not know what the squire told you, but I am a virtuous woman and I will not be bought! Not by the squire, not by you or any other man, no matter what straits of desperation you try to bring me to." Her voice quavered a little and broke.

There was a long silence in the upstairs room. The wind whistled around the eaves, rattling the window panes. Ellie sat on the hard stool, her shawl wrapped around her defensively, staring defiantly across the room at him. She swallowed. She had no idea of what she might be forced to do to keep Amy safe, but she had not reached that point. Yet.

He stared back at her, an unreadable expression on his face. Finally he spoke. "I have no idea what this conversation is about… I think whoever hit me over the head—was it you?"

She shook her head.

"That's a relief, then," he said wryly. "But whoever it was made a good job of it. My brain is quite scrambled. I have no idea what you are talking of. I cannot think straight at all. And my head feels as if it's about to split open." He stood and made to take a step, then swayed and went suddenly pale.

Without thinking she jumped up and hurried to help. "Put your head down between your knees." She pushed him gently into position. "It will help the dizziness."

After a few moments he recovered enough to lie back on the bed. He was still as pale as paper. Ellie tucked blankets around him, all thought of throwing him out forgotten. Whether he owned the cottage or not, whether he thought her a doxy or not, she could not push a sick man out into such weather. She could, however, send for his relatives.

"Who are you?" she said when he was settled against the pillows. "What's your name?"

He looked blank for a moment, then his eyes narrowed. "You tell me," he said slowly. "I told you my brain was all scrambled."

"Don't be silly. Who are you?" She leaned forward intently, awaiting his reply.

He stared at her, his blue eyes dark and intense against his stark white pallor. There was a long silence as his gaze bored into her. And then he answered.

"I am your husband."

Chapter Two

Ellie stirred the porridge angrily. The cheek of him! *I am your husband.* Why would he say such an outlandish thing? To her, of all people! He'd sounded quite sure of it, too, even a little surprised, as if wondering why she had asked him. And then he'd lain back on the bed as if too exhausted to speak any further.

She spooned the thick oatmeal porridge into two bowls and set one before Amy.

"Sugar?" the little girl asked hopefully.

"Sorry, darling. There's no sugar left." Ellie poured milk on to her daughter's bowl, and watched her daughter make islands and oceans out of porridge and milk. Gone were the days of silver dishes on the sideboard, containing every imaginable delicacy.

She picked up the other bowl. "I'll take this to the man upstairs." She took a deep breath and mounted the stairs. *I am your husband.* Indeed!

He was awake when she entered the room, his blue eyes sombre.

"How is your head?" She kept her tone brusque, impersonal.

He grimaced.

"I have brought you some porridge. Can you sit up?" She made no move to help him. She would have no truck with his nonsense. He had disturbed her quite enough as it was.

He sat up slowly. She could see from the sharp white lines around his mouth that he was in pain. She said nothing, set the bowl down with something of a snap and helped him to arrange the pillows behind him. She tried to remain indifferent, but it was not possible to avoid touching him. Each time her hand came in contact with his skin, or brushed across his warm, naked torso, she felt it, clear through to the soles of her feet. And in less acceptable regions.

He knew it, too, the devil! He'd looked up at her in such an intimate, knowing way! How dare he embarrass her any further! She ripped a blanket off the bed and flung it around his naked back and chest, then she thrust the bowl and spoon at him. "Eat."

"Yes, Mrs. Carmichael," he said in a tone of crushed obedience.

She glanced at him in suspicion. His blue, blue eyes caressed her boldly. She glared at him, then began to tidy the room briskly.

"You're gorgeous when you're angry," he said in a deep, low voice and as her breath hissed in fury, he applied himself in a leisurely manner to the porridge.

By the time she went up again to fetch his empty bowl, her wrath had dissipated. She was now more puzzled than angry. His behaviour made little sense. Why lie to her, when she was the one person in the world who would know it was a lie? And though he was teasing her now, he hadn't been teasing when he'd claimed to be her husband. It was all very odd. She decided to ask him, straight out.

"What is your name—no nonsense now. I want the truth, if you please." She took his bowl and stood looking down at him.

There was a long pause. Finally he said, "I don't know."

He said it with no inflexion at all. Ellie stared at him, and suddenly she knew he was telling the truth. "You mean you cannot remember who you are?"

"No."

Ellie was stunned. She sat down beside him on the edge of the bed, quite forgetting her resolve to keep her distance. She had heard tales of people who had lost their memories, but she had never thought to meet one. "You cannot remember *anything* about yourself?"

"No. All morning I have tried and tried, but I cannot think straight. I have no idea what my name is, nor anything about my family, or what I do for a living, or even how I came to be here." He smiled, a little sheepishly. "So you will have to tell me everything."

"But I don't know myself!"

He patted her knee and she skittered away. "No, not how I came to be hurt, but the rest. My name and all the rest."

"If you cannot remember anything, then why did you say you were my husband?"

He frowned at the accusing note in her voice and said teasingly, "Am I not your husband, then?"

"You *know* you are not."

He blinked at her in amazement. "You cannot mean it! But I thought—"

Ellie shook her head.

He considered her words for a moment and his frown grew. "But if Amy is my daughter…"

"She is no such thing!" Ellie gasped, and jumped up, horrified. "I just said you were not my husband. How dare you suggest—?"

"Then why does she call me Papa?"

"You mean—? Oh…" She sank back down on the bed. "That explains a good deal." She turned to him and said slowly, "Amy's papa, my husband, Hartley Carmichael, died a year ago. She was just a little girl and she doesn't quite remember him…" It was too difficult to explain, she realised. She finished lamely, "You have blue eyes, like her papa. And her."

"That doesn't explain how you and I came to be sharing a b—"

She knew what he was thinking and interrupted, "I never saw you before in my life until two nights ago when you arrived at my door, bleeding and frozen half-solid."

"What!"

She stood up and added in a wooden little voice, "There is only one bed big enough for an adult. It was a bitter night, one of the coldest I can recall. You were hurt and in danger of freezing to death. I could not leave you on the floor." She was unable to meet his eyes. "And as I did not want to freeze to death myself, I shared my bed with a stranger."

She flushed, recalling how the stranger had found her in his bed this morning. She had responded wantonly to his caresses. She did not blame him for thinking her a fallen woman. Her voice shook. She did not expect him to believe her, but forced herself to add, "You are the only man I have ever shared a bed with. Except for my husband, of course."

She could stay in the room no longer, with those eyes boring into her. She couldn't meet their icy blaze, couldn't bear to see the look in them. She snatched up the bowl and ran downstairs.

He watched her go, his head splitting, his mind a whirl. They were strangers? Then why would he feel this ease in her company, this sense of belonging? She didn't feel like a stranger. He'd never felt so right, so much at home as he had in bed that morning, bringing Ellie to sweet, sensual wakefulness…as if she were a part of him.

Unanswered questions gnawed at his vitals like rats. What the devil was his name? It seemed to be floating somewhere just beyond him…hovering there, on the tip of his tongue…but each time he tried for it, it drifted out of reach. He tried some names, hoping one would leap out at him, bringing the rest of his identity tumbling with him. Abraham…Allan…Adam… Was he an Adam, perhaps? He tasted it on his tongue. Familiar, yet also strange.

Bruce…David…Daniel… Was he trapped in the lion's den? He smiled and wriggled lower in the bed. His Ellie could be a little lioness when roused… She'd certainly roused him. Edward…Gilbert…James… He pulled the bedclothes around him. He could smell Ellie on them. He inhaled deeply and felt his body respond instantly. Walter…William… He dozed.

"Hello, Papa." A little voice pulled him back from the brink of sleep. He opened his eyes. A pair of big blue eyes regarded him seriously across an old cheese box.

"Hello, Amy." He sat up, drawing the sheets up with him, across his chest.

"Does your head hurt a lot?"

The headache had dwindled to a dull thump. "No, it feels a lot better, thank you."

"Mama says you don't know who you are."

He grimaced ruefully. "That's right. I can't even remember my name. I don't suppose you know my name, do you?" He tensed when the child unexpectedly nodded her head. Had Ellie not told him the truth after all? He'd had a feeling she was hiding something.

The little girl carefully put the cheese box on to the bed and then climbed up after it. She sat cross-legged and regarded him solemnly. "I think your name might be…" Her big blue eyes skimmed his chin, the top of his chest and along his arms.

He had not the faintest notion of what she found so interesting.

"Your name is…" She leaned forward and hesitantly touched his jaw and giggled. She sat back, her eyes full of mischief and said, "I think your name is…Mr. Bruin."

"Mr. Bruin?" He frowned. Bruin meant bear. "Mr. Bear?"

"Yes, because you are big and even your face is hairy." The little girl chortled in glee. "Just like a bear!"

He had to laugh at her neat trick. So, he looked like a big hairy bear to a little girl, did he? He ran a hand over his jaw. Maybe she was right. He did need a shave.

"If you think I'm a bear, then why did you call me Papa?"

She glanced guilty at the doorway. "Mama says I'm not s'posed to call you that. You won't tell, will you?"

"No, I won't tell." Again he wondered what Mama was trying to hide.

She beamed at him.

"But if your mama does not like you to call me Papa, maybe you could call me Mr. Bruin instead." It was better than having no name at all.

Her face screwed in thought, then she nodded. "Yes, that will be a good game. And you can call me Princess Amy. Do you like dolls, Mr. Bruin? I hope you don't eat them."

He resigned himself to being a little girl's playmate for the afternoon. It was better than cudgelling his aching brain for information which would not come, he supposed.

"Oh, no," he said firmly. "We bears never eat dolls."

She looked at him suspiciously. "Bears might eat *my* dolls—my dolls are very special dolls. The type which are delicious to bears."

He heaved a huge regretful sigh. "Oh, very well, you have caught me there. I solemnly promise never to eat Princess Amy's Very Special Dolls."

"Good." She snuggled closer to him, pulled the box on to his knees and began to introduce her dolls to him.

The cheese box was a home-made dolls' house, he realised. Everything in it was made by clumsy small fingers or her mother's neat touch. And some of her dolls were made of acorns, with cradles and all sorts of minia-ture items made of acorn caps and walnut shells.

He smiled to himself. Delicious to bears, indeed. She was a delightful child. Her eyes were such a bright blue…almost the exact same colour as his. It was a most discomforting thought. He hoped Ellie had not lied about Amy's parent-age. If he had created this charming child with Ellie…and left her to grow up without his name, in what looked to him a lot like poverty…then he didn't much like himself.

All thoughts led to the same question—who the devil was he? And was he already married?

* * *

"He was so badly hurt he now cannot remember a thing," explained Ellie to the one person who could be trusted not to tell the squire of her unexpected houseguest.

"It's an absolute disgrace!" The vicar paced the floor in agitation. "That gang of robbers is getting bolder and bolder and will the squire do a thing about it? No—he is much too indolent to bother! He ought to close down the Angel. I'm sure that den of iniquity is their headquarters. Can your fellow identify any of the miscreants?"

"No, he doesn't even know his own name, let alone anything that happened."

The elderly vicar pursed his lips thoughtfully. "And there was nothing on his person to indicate his identity?"

Ellie shook her head. "Nothing. Whoever robbed him had stripped him of even his coat and shoes. I thought you may have heard something."

"No. No one has made enquiries. Er…he is not causing you any, er, difficulty?"

"No, he has been a gentleman the entire time…" Except for where his hands had roamed this morning, she thought, fighting the blush. The vicar had no idea of the sleeping arrangements at her cottage, otherwise he wouldn't have countenanced it for a moment.

The vicar frowned suddenly and glanced around. "Where is little Miss Amy?"

"I left her at the cottage. It is very bitter out and she had a bad cold which she has only just recovered from. It…it was only for a few minutes…" Her voice trailed off.

"You left her alone with this stranger?" He sounded incredulous.

Ellie felt suddenly foolish. Criminally foolish. "I didn't

think…I don't *feel* as though he would hurt Amy—or me." She bit her lip in distress. "But… you're right. He could be a murderer, for all I know."

The vicar said doubtfully. "I'm sure there's nothing to worry about. If you'd had doubts about this fellow, you'd have brought Amy with you. You have good instincts."

With every comforting word, Ellie's doubts grew. As did her anxiety.

He nodded. "You are having second thoughts. Leave this matter in my hands. If a man has gone missing, we shall eventually hear something. Go home, my dear. See to your child."

"Oh, yes. Yes, I will. Thank you for the loan of these items, Vicar." She lifted the small packet in her hand. "I shall return them shortly."

Ellie ran most of the way home, her fears growing by the minute. How could she have let her…her feelings, outweigh her common sense! Leaving Amy behind, just because it was cold and damp outside! Taking a man's word for it that he recalled nothing. Assuming that simply because she liked him—liked him far too much, in fact—that he was therefore trustworthy. For all she knew, he could be the veriest villain!

It was all very well for the vicar to talk of her instincts being sound, but he didn't know of the mess she had made of her life. She trusted her instincts and her feelings as far as she could throw them. Which was not at all! Dear Lord, she had left her daughter with a complete stranger! If anything happened to Amy, she couldn't bear it.

She raced to the cottage and flung open the door. The downstairs room was empty. No sign of her daughter. She heard voices above her. She could not make out what was being said. Then she heard a small anxious squeak.

"No, no! Stop that!" Amy shrieked.

Ellie raced up the steep stairs, taking them two at a time, almost tripping on her skirts as she did. She hurtled into the room and stood there, gasping for breath, staring at the sight which greeted her.

The murderer she had left her daughter with was sitting in her bed where she had left him. He had found his shirt, thank goodness, and wore it now, covering that broad, disturbing chest. He was also wearing one of her shawls and her best bonnet, albeit crookedly, its ribbons tied in a clumsy bow across his stubble-roughened jaw. His arms were full of dolls. Across his lap, over the bedclothes, a tea towel had been laid and on it, a diminutive tea party was set out, with pretend food and drink in acorn-cap bowls.

He met Ellie's gaze rather sheepishly, his blue eyes twinkling in wry humour.

"Oh, Mama, Mr. Bruin keeps moving and spilling my dolls' picnic. Look!" Amy crossly displayed several tipped-over bowls. "Bad Mr. Bruin!" the little girl said severely.

"I'm sorry, Princess Amy, but I did warn you that we bears are great clumsy beasts and not fit company for a picnic with ladies," responded Ellie's murderer apologetically.

Ellie burst into tears.

There was a shocked silence. "Mama, what is it? What's the matter?" Amy scrambled off the bed and threw her arms around her mother's legs tightly.

Ellie sat down on the stool, pulled Amy into her arms and hugged her tightly, tucking the child into her body, rocking her. The sobs kept coming. Hard, painful, from deep in her chest. She couldn't stop them.

She heard movement from the direction of the bed, but the weeping had taken hold of her. She could do nothing but hold her daughter and let the tears come. She knew it was weak, knew it was spineless of her, that she was supposed to be strong and look after Amy…Amy, who was now sobbing in fright because she had never seen her mother cry before…

But Ellie could not control the harsh sobs. They came from somewhere deep inside her, wrenching painfully out of her body, almost choking her. She had never cried like this before. It was terrifying.

In a vague way, she sensed him standing beside her. She thought she felt a few awkward pats on her shoulder and back, but she couldn't be sure. Suddenly she felt powerful arms scoop her up. He lifted both her and Amy and carried them back to the bed and sat down, holding them on his lap, in the circle of his arms, hard against his big, warm chest. Ellie tried to resist, but feebly and after a moment or two, something inside her, some barrier, just…dissolved and she relaxed against him, letting herself be held in a way she had never in her life been held. The sobs came even harder then.

He asked no questions, just held them, nuzzling Ellie's hair with his jaw and cheek, making soothing sounds. Amy stopped crying almost immediately. After a moment, Ellie heard him whisper to her daughter to go and wash her face, that Mama would be all right soon, that she was just tired. She felt her daughter slip out of her grasp. Amy leaned against his knee and waited anxiously, patting and stroking her mother's heaving shoulders.

Ellie forced herself to smile in a way she hoped would reassure the little girl. She tried desperately to get control of her emotions, but she couldn't yet speak—she was breathing in jerky gasps, gulping and snuffling in an ugly fashion. Sobs welled up intermittently; dry, painful shuddery eruptions. She heard Amy tiptoe downstairs.

Finally, the last of the frightful, frightening outburst passed. Ellie was exhausted, with as much energy as a wet rag—and feeling about as attractive.

"I…I'm sorry about that," she said gruffly. "I…I don't know what came over me."

"Hush, now. It doesn't matter." His arms were warm and steady around her. He smoothed a damp curl back from her face.

"I'm not usually such a dreadful watering pot, really I'm not."

"I know." His voice was deep and soft in her ear.

"It was just…I suddenly got the idea—I mean, I thought…" How could she tell him what she'd thought? What could she say? I thought you were going to hurt my daughter and when I found you hadn't, I burst into tears all over you instead. How ridiculous was that? He would think she belonged in Bedlam. She wasn't sure herself that she didn't belong there!

"I've never cried like that in my life. Not even when my husband died."

"Then you were well overdue for it. Don't refine too much on it," he said in a matter-of-fact voice. "No doubt you were at the end of your tether and things had built up inside you until there was no bearing it. When that happens, you have to let it out somehow."

She made a small gesture of repudiation of his words and he went on, "Women cry, men usually get into a fight, or—" she felt the smile in his voice "—take to the bedchamber. But I have seen men weep and weep, just like you did when things have got too much to bear. There is no shame in it."

There was a small silence. "Have you wept like that?"

She felt him tense. He said nothing for a long moment and then shook his head. "No, blast it! I still cannot recall. I thought I had it for a minute." He sighed and she felt his warm breath in her hair. "It is so frustrating, as if it's all there, waiting. Like something half glimpsed in the corner of my eye and when I turn my head to look at it directly, it is gone…"

She laid her hand on his. "It will come soon, I am certain of it."

"That's as may be. Now, do you want to talk about it?"

"About what?"

He turned her in his arms so that she could see his face properly. "Don't prevaricate. What was it that so upset you? Tell me. I might not be able to remember anything, but I'll help you in any way I can. Did someone try to hurt you?" His voice was deep and sincere.

Ellie couldn't bring herself to confess the ugly suspicion that had crept over her at the vicarage. She looked at him, trying to think of how she could explain…

Her face must have shown more than she realised.

"It's me, isn't it?" he said softly. "I'm your problem."

She said nothing for a moment, but he knew it anyway. His hands dropped away and suddenly she felt cold. He gently lifted her off his lap and placed her on the bed beside him.

"No, no," she said hurriedly. "It's—there are so many problems and difficulties, but I don't want to burden—"

"Just tell me this—I…I need to know it." His voice was

a little hoarse. "Do you *truly* not know me, or do you know me and…and fear me for some reason?"

There was a short silence, then he reached down beneath the mattress and drew out the frying pan she had placed there on the first night.

Ellie reddened. She didn't know where to look.

"I found it this morning, as I was getting dressed. This was for me, wasn't it? In case I attacked you in the night."

Ellie nodded, embarrassed.

"And when you came rushing in here just now, having run a mile or more…I was the reason. You were worried about Amy, weren't you? About leaving her alone with me. And when you found her safe and…untouched, you burst into tears of relief…"

Ellie was miserably silent.

His fist curled into a knot of tension at her unspoken confirmation of his theory. "I cannot blame you for it. We neither of us have any notion of the sort of man I am. I do not *believe* I would harm a child…but until I get my memory back, I cannot *know* what sort of man I am…or have been." Frustration and distress were evident in his voice.

Ellie tried to think of what to say. He was a good man, she felt it in her bones. But he was right. They didn't know anything about him.

"I suppose I made the situation worse, grabbing you like that," he said bitterly. "I didn't know what to do. I just needed to hold you… I see now it was presumptuous of me."

Ellie wanted to cry out, No! She wanted to tell him that he had done exactly the right thing, that she had derived such comfort from being held that it was too embarrassing to admit. She couldn't explain how in his embrace she had discovered the release of being weak for once…even for a short while. All her life she had had to be the strong one.

She wanted to tell him how wonderful it had been to be held by a strong man as if she were precious, as if he cherished her…despite her weakness.

But she could not expose such vulnerability to him. Men exploited a woman's vulnerability. And God help her, she was coming to care for him—much more than was reasonable—a nameless stranger she had known two nights and two days, and most of that with him insensible. She could not let him know that about her.

"And for this morning…in bed…I also apologise."

Ellie's face flamed. She scrambled to her feet. "There's nothing to apologise for," she said huskily. "We were both half-asleep and you cannot be held responsible for…for what you did. You did not know what you were—"

"Yes, I did," he interrupted her in a deep voice. "I knew exactly what I was doing. And I give you fair warning, Mrs. Carmichael. While my memory is impaired, your virtue is safe with me. But the moment I discover who I am, and whether I am married or not…"

She waited for him to finish his sentence and, when he did not, looked up at him anxiously.

He smiled at her in a possessive, wolfish manner and said with soft deliberation. "If I am not married, then be warned, Mrs. Ellie Carmichael…I plan to have you naked in bed with me again, doing all of those things we were doing and more." It was a vow.

Ellie's face was scarlet, but she managed to say with some composure. "I think I may have some say in that matter, sir."

"You liked it well enough this morning…"

"You have no idea what I thought!" she snapped. "And we will discuss this foolishness no further! Now, I have brought some slippers for you. The vicar's feet are too small to borrow his boots, but the slippers will do at a pinch. And there is a razor, too."

He ran a rueful hand over his jaw. "So you don't like my bristles, eh? Your daughter didn't, but I thought you may have rather enjoyed the…stimulation." He grinned at her, a thoroughly wicked twinkle in those impossibly blue eyes.

"Enough!" said Ellie briskly, thinking her whole body must have turned scarlet by now. "I shall fetch hot water for you to shave and then we shall dine. There is hare stew in the pot."

"Yes, the smell has been tantalising me for some time." His eyes were warm upon her. "There are so many tantalising things in this cottage, a hungry fellow like me has no chance…" His eyes told her exactly what he meant by "hungry." And it wasn't about stew.

She fled.

"Mama sent me up with her looking glass," announced Amy from the doorway. "She says you will need it to shave."

He grinned. A few minutes earlier, Mama had poked her head in the room, dumped a pot of hot water just inside the doorway and disappeared again, muttering things about having work to do. He probably shouldn't have taken off his shirt, but he was damned if he was going to shave in the only shirt he apparently owned.

Amy handed him the small, square looking glass and

he took it gingerly, suddenly unnerved by the prospect of his own reflection. Would he recognise himself?

He lifted the glass slowly and grimaced. No wonder she didn't trust him an inch! He was a bloody pirate! All that was missing was the gold earring and the eyepatch! His skin was dark—tanned by weather, he decided, comparing it with other parts of his body. So he lived a lot out of doors. Gentlemen didn't do that. Pirates, however…

His eyes were blue, but then he knew that earlier from the little girl watching him so solemnly. No wonder she'd thought him a bear, though—he didn't just need a shave, he needed a haircut as well. Under the bandage, his hair was thick and dark and unruly. His brows were thick and black and frowning like the devil. His nose was long and—he turned his head slightly—not quite straight. He'd broken his nose at some time. And his skin carried several small scars as well as the remains of recent bruises. All in all, not a pretty sight. He'd found old scars on his body, too. He'd been in more than his share of fights.

A fine fellow for a woman to take in and care for—a brawling, hairy, black-bearded pirate! He wouldn't have blamed anyone for leaving such a villainous creature out in the cold, let alone an unprotected woman with a small daughter. He reached for the hot water and soap. At least he could take care of the beard.

"Will you hold the looking glass for me, please, Princess?"

Eagerly Amy took it and watched, fascinated, as he soaped up his skin and then carefully shaved the soap and beard off.

"Better?" he asked when he'd finished.

She reached out and passed a small soft palm over the

newly shaven skin. "Nice," she said consideringly, "but I liked Mr. Bruin's prickles, too."

He chuckled. "Prickly bears don't belong in cottages. Now, I'm going to finish washing, so you pop downstairs, Princess, and help your mother. I'll be down shortly."

Ellie's throat went dry. She tried to swallow as he bent his head under the low beam and came down the last few steps. He suddenly looked so...different. Freshly shaved, he had removed the bandage and combed his hair neatly back with water. His skin glowed with health, his eyes were bright and lit with a lurking devilish gleam. His clean white shirt seemed to shine against his tanned skin; the sleeves were rolled back almost to his elbow. The shirt was tucked into buckskin breeches, not quite skin-tight, but nevertheless...

It was foolish, she told herself severely. They must have been tight when he arrived, too—in fact, tighter, because he was drenched. It was knowing the body beneath the buckskins, knowing it had been pressed against her, naked, only this morning, which was creating this unwanted heat in the pit of her stomach.

"Sit down. The table is set." She gestured and turned back to the fire to lift off the heavy pot of bubbling stew.

A brawny arm wrapped itself around her waist, while with his other hand, he whisked the cloth pad from her hand and used it to lift the black cast-iron pot off its hook.

"I can do that," she muttered, wriggling out of his light clasp.

"I know. But I've caused you enough work. While I'm here, I'll lighten your load as much as possible." He carried the pot carefully to the table.

While I'm here... The words echoed in her head. Yes, as soon as he recovered his memory, he would be off, no doubt, back to his wife and children. All twelve of them, she thought glumly.

They ate in silence. He ate neatly and without fuss. He passed her the bread and the salt and refilled her cup of water without being asked. Ellie pondered as she ate. His manners and his accent suggested he was gently bred, but his body bore the signs of one who had led a very physically challenging existence. He was also familiar with the workings of a cottage hearth; he deftly swapped the stewing pot with the large water kettle, rebuilt the fire in a manner which revealed he knew not to squander her precious fuel and generally showed himself to be at home in her meagre surroundings—as no gentleman would be. A servant might acquire table manners and an accent, but he showed none of the servility of a man who had been in service. On the contrary, he was rather arrogant in the way he simply did what he wished, whether she wanted to be helped or not.

He fixed a loose shutter. The banging had driven her mad most of the year, but somehow, his fixing it—without saying a word to her—annoyed her. He went outside into the cold, despite his lack of coat, and chopped her a huge pile of wood, stacking it under the eaves at the back door which was much more convenient than where she had stored her wood before. He swung the axe with ease and familiarity. And his muscles rippled beneath the loose, soft shirt in a way that dried her mouth. Her eyes clung to his form like ivy to a rock...until she remembered to go on with what she had been doing. She should have been grateful for his help. She was grateful...only...

Any minute now he would remember his name and that he had a wife who had a right to command these services from him! And twelve children. How dare he make himself indispensable…making her and Amy feel like they were part of a family… It wasn't fair.

In the afternoon she'd seen Amy standing outside looking up, her little face pale and stiff with fear. Ellie had rushed out to see what was happening, only to rival her daughter in fear as she watched the wretched man clambering about on her steep roof, replacing and adjusting slates as if he hadn't a care in the world. She stood there, twisting a tea-towel helplessly in her hands, watching. Several times his foot slipped and her heart leapt right out of her chest and lodged as a hard lump in her throat as she realised he was fixing her leaking roof. He must have noticed the pot she placed in the corner of her room to catch the drips.

She hadn't breathed a scrap of air the whole time he was up there, and how he'd got up there without a ladder she didn't even want to think about! But when he'd come down finally in a rush which left her gasping in fright, and then he'd stood there, with that…that *look* in his eye, as if she should be pleased he'd risked his fool neck for such a trivial matter, well!

She'd wanted to throttle him there and then. Or jump on him and kiss him senseless.

But of course, she couldn't do any of that, because he wasn't hers to kiss or throttle and he probably never would be. She couldn't even yell at him, because how could she possibly yell at him for helping her? For scaring her silly? For making her realise that she loved him? The wretch!

She loved him.

The triumphant grin died slowly from his face and a light came into his eyes that made Ellie wonder whether she had said the words aloud. He stared at her, burning with intensity, his blue eyes blazing at whatever he read in her face. He strode towards her purposefully. She knew he was going to gather her up in his arms and kiss her like he had in the morning, in that way that melted her very bones.

But she could not, oh, she could not. For if she let him love her she could not bear it if she had to let him go… She held a shaking hand up to stop him and he came to a halt a scant pace away. His eyes devoured her, his chest heaving. Her eyes clung to him, even as her hands warded him off. They stood there, unmoving.

"Mr. Bruin!" said a cross little voice.

He ignored it, staring at Ellie, eating her up with his eyes.

"Mr. Bruin!" Amy tugged furiously at his buckskin breeches.

With a visible effort, he finally tore his gaze from Ellie and squatted down in front of her daughter. "What is it, Princess?"

"You are *not* allowed to climb up on the roof without askin' Mama! It's very dangerous. You could've fallen down and broken your head again. You're a bad bear!" Her voice quivered as she added, "And you frightened me and Mama terrible bad."

His voice softened. "Did I, Princess? I'm very sorry, then." And he gathered the little girl into his arms and hugged her gently. His eyes met Ellie's across the little girl's head, filled with contrition and some nameless emotion.

Ellie's eyes misted. What was she to do with a man like this? How could any woman not love him? She turned back to the cottage. He probably had half a dozen adoring wives.

Ellie was jumpy. The night was closing in on her. They sat by the fire in companionable silence. She was mending, he was whittling at a stick. Amy had gone to bed some time before. It was long past Ellie's bedtime too, but she had been putting off the moment. They would share a bed again soon. There was no choice. Of course, they had shared a bed for the last two nights, but he had been mostly unconscious. Mostly...

She kept trying not to think about the feeling of waking up in his embrace. She could not allow it to happen again. It was unseemly behaviour in a respectable widow and she would have no part of it. Besides, she feared if she allowed him to touch her like that again, there could be no stopping. She had already fallen more than halfway in love with him. If she gave herself to him she knew she would be letting him into her heart as well as her body...

She'd lost almost everything in her life as it was, but she had survived the loss. If she let herself love him and then lost him, it might be the loss she could not bear. For Amy's sake, if not for her own, she had to keep herself strong. She could not afford to break her heart. She would not *let* him break her heart.

She cleared her throat. "Mr. Bruin." She had taken to using Amy's name for him.

He looked up. "Mrs. Carmichael?" A slow smile crinkled across his face, white teeth gleaming wolfishly in the firelight. He had that look in his eye again. She felt her pulse flutter.

"It is about the sleeping arrangements," she said in an attempt to sound brisk and matter of fact. It came out as something of a squeak.

"Yes?" His voice deepened.

"I am a virtuous widow," she began.

He raised an eyebrow.

"I am—" she repeated indignantly.

"It's all right, love," he said. "I am not doubting your virtue."

"Don't call me lo—"

He held up his hand pacifically. "Mrs. Carmichael… Ellie…your virtue is safe with me. On my honour as a gentleman, I will do nothing to cause you distress."

Ellie looked troubled. It was all very well for him to make a noble-sounding promise, but how did either of them know he *was* a gentleman? And what did causing her distress mean? His leaving would cause her distress, but would he stay, once he recovered his wits? She doubted it. Why would a handsome man in the peak of health and fitness want to stay in a small cottage in the middle of nowhere with a poverty-stricken widow and a small girl?

"There is no choice but to…" she swallowed convulsively "…share a bed, but that is as far as it goes. I will wrap myself entirely in a sheet and you shall do the same. And thus we may share a bed and blankets, but remain chaste. Are you agreed?" Her voice squeaked again.

He bowed ironically. "I am agreed. Now, shall I go up and disrobe while you do the same down here with the fire?"

Ellie felt herself go hot. "Very well." She fetched down her thickest nightgown and, the moment she heard his footstep overhead, began to unbutton her dress. She undressed in the firelight, glancing once or twice at the window, at the black, opaque night outside, feeling exposed. Wrapping her thickest shawl around her, she took a candle and hurried upstairs. On the threshold she paused.

"Did you find your sheet?" she whispered. "I put it on the bed for you."

A deep chuckle answered her. The sound shivered through her bones deliciously.

"Did you?" she repeated, lifting the candle to peer into the sleeping alcove.

"Yes, love. I gave my word, remember. I'm as chaste as a bug in a rug." His bare upper chest and shoulders glowed dark against the white sheet. His eyes were deep shadows of mystery, and his white teeth gleamed briefly. He didn't look chaste. He looked handsome and powerful and altogether far too appealing for a virtuous widow's peace of mind.

She swallowed and turning her back, sat down to remove her shoes and stockings. Then she picked up her own sheet and wrapped herself tightly in it, feeling his eyes watching her every movement. Finally she blew out the candle, set it on the floor next to the bed, took a deep breath and slipped in beside him.

She lay stiffly on her back, huddled beneath the blankets in the cocoon of her sheet, trying not to touch him. All she could hear was the wind in the trees and the breathing of the man beside her. It was worse than the first time she had slept with him. Then she'd feared him as a stranger. Now the danger he represented was not the sort that a frying pan could fix.

Before, he had been a stranger to her, nothing more

than a wounded, beautiful body. Now she knew how his eyes could dance, what he tasted like, how his hands felt moving over her skin, caressing her as if she was beautiful to him, precious. Before her marriage, men had only wanted her for her inheritance. Now she had nothing to offer a man except herself. And yet this man in her bed wanted her. And when he touched her she felt…cherished.

It was dangerously seductive. He had already found his way under her skin, if not her skirts. Now, all she had was a thin cotton sheet to protect her virtue—and her heart. She lay rigid, hardly daring to breathe.

"Oh, for heaven's sake!" With a surge of bedclothes he turned, flipped her on her side and pulled her into the curve of his body.

"Stop it! You promised—"

"And I do not break my promises! This is as chaste as I can manage it. Now stop fussing, Ellie. There is a sheet wrapped around each of us—it is perfectly decorous. But I cannot possibly sleep while you lie there as stiff as a board…" He chuckled awkwardly. "That's my problem, too, if you want to know."

Ellie buried her hot cheek in her cool pillow. No, she didn't want to know that. It was bad enough that she could feel his problem, even through the sheets. The feel of him set off all sorts of reactions in her own body.

"I'm sorry, I shouldn't have said that. Now, stop worrying, love, and go to sleep. We'll both rest better like this, you know it."

Ellie did not know it, but she allowed herself to remain in the curve of his body, enjoying the warmth of him and the feeling of strength and protection which emanated from him. It was a strange and seductive sensation, this feeling of being…cherished.

They lay in silence for a long time, listening to the wind in the trees. And finally, Ellie slept.

He lay in the dark, holding Ellie against the length of his body. Even through the sheets wound around them, he could feel her soft curves, curled trustfully against him. Her feet had kicked free of their cotton shroud and tucked themselves between his calves, like two cold little stones. He smiled in the dark. He was happy to be her personal hot brick.

She sighed in her sleep and snuggled closer to him. He buried his face in the nape of her neck. He laid his mouth on her skin and tasted her gently with his tongue. Her scent was unique, like fresh harvested wheat…like bread dough, before it was baked…and hay as it was scythed. Fresh and good. He felt as if the fragrance of her skin had become a part of him.

Who the devil was he? It was unbearable to be so helpless, to be imprisoned in the dark, unable to make decisions about his life. How the hell could he plan any sort of a future when his past was a blank slate?

And what if his memory failed to return? Would he be forever hamstrung by self-ignorance? And if his memory didn't come back, how long could he stay here with Ellie? He couldn't ask her to support him. Yet he couldn't continue to live with her—a few days in winter they might get away with, but much more and her reputation would be compromised. And Ellie was a woman who valued her reputation. He inhaled the scent of her. He must not damage her. Must not let her be hurt by his situation. But how?

Questions continued to rattle fruitlessly in his head, until at last he fell asleep.

When he awoke Ellie was wrapped around him. They were lying face to face. Or rather her face to his chest. She was using him as a pillow. Warm little puffs of air warmed his chest as she breathed. Her hair, loosened from its braid, flowed in waves over his skin. One of her hands was curled around his neck, the other was draped across his chest. The sheets they had been wrapped so chastely in were now bundled ineffectively around their middles, leaving them uncovered above and below. There was nothing chaste about their current positions.

The warm soft weight of her against his naked skin was irresistibly appealing. He stifled a moan. He was rock hard and aching from wanting her. Her legs were twined around his, one leg over his hip. She was open to him. One small movement and he could be inside her. He had never wanted anything so much. She was his woman, his heart-mate and she was soft, sleepy and open to him.

He swallowed hard. He wanted so badly, needed so much, to be inside her. His entire body throbbed with the need. He fought it. He had given his word. She trusted him. He might be a nameless pirate, but he had given his word and she'd believed him.

He would not take her, but that didn't mean he had to be a saint. He ran his hand down her body. The sheets were bunched around her middle, riding up over her thighs. He ran his hand along the leg she'd thrown across his hip, caressed her sweetly rounded backside, hesitated, then stroked the silken skin of her belly and thighs. She was warm, sweet and more than ready for him. A hard shudder rocked his body. He closed his eyes, willing the need back down.

He must have awoken her. Eyes still closed, she stretched languidly and the need rocked through him, almost shattering his fragile self-control. She moved her legs against his and he tried unsuccessfully to close his mind against the delicious friction of her soft skin rubbing against his.

Sleepily, she opened her eyes and looked at him, blinking drowsily. Still barely awake, she smiled at him. Her skin was flushed a soft pink, her lips were parted and damp and smiling in welcome. His hand moved again, caressing her intimately and her eyes widened in shock, even as her body arched towards him. He had not broken his word, but he was perilously close to it. He removed his hand.

She moved back in sudden caution, only to find her legs were gripping him.

"Oh!" she exclaimed and tried to untangle herself from him. He watched her sweet embarrassment as she discovered her sheet and nightgown pushed up to her middle, and the extremely intimate position they were in. She struggled to pull the sheet and nightgown down and in the process her hand brushed against his arousal.

She froze as she realised what she'd done and he gritted his teeth, willing control. Her face flamed adorably and she avoided his eyes in sudden shyness. It was odd for a married woman with a child to be so shy, but he had no time to explore that question. His focus was on the battle between his body and his mind. His body wanted nothing more than to make love to her. His mind also wanted it, heart and soul.

But for a man who had no memories, one single extremely inconvenient memory remained: *"your virtue is safe with me. On my honour as a gentleman, I will do nothing to cause you distress…"*

Again, she tugged surreptitiously at the hem of her nightgown, and again, she brushed up against him. Another encounter and he would not be answerable for the consequences. He reached down and lifted her hands away from the danger zone.

"Don't worry about it, Ellie. These things happen," he said softly. "I haven't forgotten my promise. Good morning," he added, and kissed her.

Recalling her earlier shyness, he planned to make it a gentle, tender, unthreatening kiss, but as her mouth opened under his and he tasted her sweet, tart, sleepy mouth, he was lost.

Their second kiss was more passionate.

He kissed her a third time and felt at the end of it that his body was about to explode. He raised his head, like a drowning man going down for the last time, and said softly, "Three is my limit, Mrs. Carmichael."

She blinked at him, her eyes wide and dazed looking, her lips slightly swollen from his kisses. She gazed into his eyes, as if reading his soul. He wondered what he saw in him but was distracted when her eyes dropped.

"Three?" she whispered vaguely. Staring hungrily at his mouth, she licked her lips.

He groaned. She didn't understand. He was poised on the brink. If she didn't get out of bed now, he would be lost. "Three kisses. If I kiss you again, I fear I will forget my promise to you." She frowned, so he reminded her. "My promise that your virtue would be safe with me," and added ironically, "*on my honour as a gentleman*. If you are not out of this bed in one minute, I will not be answerable for the consequences."

It took a moment for her to comprehend what he was saying and he had to smile. She was even more befuddled by passion than he was. But once his meaning percolated to her brain, she gasped and scrambled hurriedly out of the bed. She stood there on the bare floor, staring, her chest heaving as if she had run a race. His own breathing was just as ragged.

"I...I am sorry," she said in a low voice and, snatching her clothes from the hook behind the door, left the room.

A moment later she was back, in the doorway, clutching her clothes against her chest, looking uncomfortable. "I...I wish...we could have...you know." She blushed rosily. "I'm sorry." She turned to go then paused and turned back, resolutely. "It was the loveliest awakening I have ever had, thank you," she said in a gruff little voice and hurried down the stairs.

He lay back in the bed, his body throbbing with unsatisfied need, a wry smile on his face. *"It was the loveliest awakening I have ever had, thank you."* It took courage for Mrs. "I-am-a-Virtuous-Widow" to admit that; courage and a kind of shy, sensual honesty that made him want to leap down the stairs after her and drag her back to bed. It would be an awakening in more ways than one, he suspected.

It would be wise to spend the day in making a straw pallet for him to sleep on during the coming night...but he had no intention of being wise. Tonight he would retract his gentlemanly promise. It didn't matter that he didn't know who he was. Whoever he was, he would make it right for her.

Tonight she would be his.

Chapter Three

Ellie swept out the ash and charcoal from last night's fire and began to set a new one, her hands moving mechanically, her mind reliving the wondrously delicious sensations she had experienced at his hands a few moments earlier. His hands… She felt herself blush, again, thinking of where his hands had been, so big and capable… touching her with such tenderness…and creating such sensations. She had never felt anything so…so…

It made her want to weep again, at the beauty of it…and the frustration.

The wood shavings which remained from his whittling smouldered, then smoked. She blew on them gently and flames licked at the wood. He'd built a fire inside her, a fire which still smouldered within her. She watched curl after curl of wood smoulder, then burst into brilliant flame. A moment of splendour, then each one crumbled into grey ash. Was that what it would be like to be possessed by him? One moment of glory, followed by a lifetime of regret? Or would it build into a more permanent fire, one with deep hot coals?

She filled the big black kettle with water and swung it on to the lowest hook. Hastily, because he might come down at any minute, she washed herself with soap and cold water and dressed before the fire. The kettle soon began to steam and she set the porridge to cook, stirring it rhythmically, her mind dreamily recalling the sensation of waking up in his arms.

Rat-tat-tat!

Ellie jumped. Someone at the door at this hour of the morning? Her eye fell on the hare skins hung up to dry on a hook near the door. Of course. Ned with the milk. She flung open the door, a smile of welcome on her face.

It froze there. "Sq…Squire Hammet."

A large burly man dressed more to suit a London afternoon promenade than a rural Northumberland morning pushed past her. His gaze raked her intimately.

Ellie shrivelled inside and braced herself. "To what do I owe this unexpected visit?"

"You've had a man here, missy!" The squire's angry gaze probed the small room.

"Why do you say that?" Ellie prayed that the floorboards overhead would not squeak.

"A man was seen on your roof yesterday." The squire thrust his red face at her. The scent of expensive pomade emanated from him, as did the faint scent of soiled linen. Like his friend, her late husband, the squire favoured expensive clothing, but disdained bathing.

Ellie turned away, trying to hide her fear and disgust. "There was a man here yesterday. He fixed the leaking roof for me."

"It's my blasted cottage! I say who fixes the roof or not! So, you have a secret fancy man do you, Miss-Prim-and-

Proper?" His face was mottled with anger. "Too high and mighty to give the time of day to me, who lent you this house out of the kindness of my heart, and now I find you've let some filthy peasant come sniffing around your skirts."

"You are disgusting!"

"Who was it, dammit—I want to know the fellow's name!"

Ellie turned angrily. "I have no idea of his name or anything about him. He merely fixed my roof for me and I gave him some food in return! I've been asking you to fix those broken slates for months now and you have done nothing!"

"Only because you have refused your part of the bargain." Small, hot eyes ran over her body lasciviously.

Ellie shuddered and forced herself to ignore it. "There was no bargain. There never will be. I pay rent on this cottage and that is the end of it."

"Pah, a peppercorn rent!"

"The rent you offered me on the day of Hart's funeral! If it was lower than usual, I did not know it at the time. I thought you were being kind because you were my husband's friend. I should have known better," she finished bitterly and turned to stir the porridge.

"You should have indeed. There's no such thing as something for nothing." The squire's voice thickened and Ellie jumped as thick, meaty hands slid around her, groping for her breasts.

"Take your hands off me!" She jerked her elbow into his stomach, hard and he gasped and released her. She whirled and pushed him hard. Off balance, he staggered back and banged his head on the shelf behind him.

She flung open the door and stood there, holding it. "You are not welcome in this cottage, sir. If I've told you once, I've told you a hundred times, I am—and shall be— no man's mistress. And even if I was so inclined, I would *never* be yours, Squire Hammet!"

The squire stood there, breathing heavily and rubbed his head. "You little vixen! I'll punish you for that, see if I don't. His eyes ran over her again. "I don't mean to leave here unsatisfied again. I had a good eyeful of you this morning and I liked what I saw."

Ellie felt ill. She never got dressed downstairs, usually. Of all the days to do it, when Squire Hammet was outside the window, watching. She glanced at the fire, to where her cast-iron poker was propped. If only she could get hold of it…

"No, you don't, vixen." The squire put his big burly body between her and the poker.

Ellie was beside the open door. She could run away into the forest and hide, but she couldn't leave Amy in the house.

The squire seemed to read her mind. "Where's that brat of yours?" He glanced around the room and his eyes came to rest on the cheese-box dolls' house. "You would not want her to…have an accident, would you?" With no warning his shiny boots stamped down on the child's toy, smashing it to bits. He kicked the shattered remains into the fire.

Ellie gasped with fright and rage. She watched the flames devour a little girl's dream world. Amy was upstairs, still asleep, she hoped. She did not want her daughter to witness what would come next. She would kill the squire before she let him touch her.

"Mama, Mama!" In bare feet and nightgown, Amy came hurtling down the stairs. She flew across the room to her mother, but in a flash the squire reached out and grabbed the child by the arm. Amy shrieked with fear and pain.

"Let go of her!" screamed Ellie.

Amy squirmed in the squire's grasp, then, unable to break free, the little girl suddenly turned and fastened her teeth in the hand of the man who held her. The squire let out a bellow of rage and Amy wriggled out of his grasp and fled.

Ellie darted forward and grabbed the poker. She lifted it, but before she could bring it down on the man's elegantly curled and pomaded head, a strong hand grabbed the squire by the collar, whirled him around and flung him across the room.

It was Mr. Bruin, dressed in nothing but a shirt and breeches, thick, dark stubble covering his jaw, blue eyes blazing with fury.

"Get out!" he said. "And if I ever find you bothering this lady again—"

"Lady!" the squire spat. "Some lady! You've obviously spent the night in her bed, but don't assume it's anything special! Half the men in the county have been under those skirts—and she's not fussy about class—in fact, she enjoys a bit of the rough—"

A big, powerful fist cut off the rest of the sentence. "Enjoy a bit of the rough, yourself, do you, Squire?" said Mr. Bruin softly, punctuating each word with a punch.

The squire was a big man, thicker and more solid in build than Mr. Bruin, but he was no match for Ellie's barefoot avenger. She winced at the sound of flesh punishing flesh, even as part of her was cheering.

"Now get out, you piece of carrion!"

The squire wheezed, sagged and scuttled out the door, looking much smaller than when he had arrived. His nose was bleeding and from the crack she'd heard, it was probably broken. His face bore numerous marks from the fight and his eyes were swollen half-closed. They would probably be black by the afternoon.

Mr. Bruin, on the other hand, was unmarked and not even winded.

"I'll have you for this!" the squire swore from a safe distance. "I'm the magistrate around here. I'll have you transported, you ruffian!"

"I'm sure the court will enjoy hearing how a lone virtuous widow and child were forced to defend themselves with a poker from the unwanted attentions of a prancing, pomaded, middle-aged Lothario. Yes, I can just see you admitting to the world you were bested by a woman, a poker and a little girl," said Ellie's defender in a deep, amused voice.

The squire swore vilely.

"Need another lesson in manners, do you, louse?" Mr. Bruin bunched his fists. "Or shall I leave you to the tender mercies of Mrs. Carmichael and her poker?"

Ellie watched as the squire fled, still cursing and muttering threats. He had made her life almost unbearable before: after this humiliation he would make it impossible. She would have to leave this place, but she didn't regret it one iota.

"That saw him off!" she said with satisfaction.

"You've dealt with this before," he said slowly.

She nodded. "He was one of my husband's closest friends, you know. When the magnitude of Hart's indebtedness became known, he offered me help." She laughed, bitterly. "I was an heiress when Hart married me. I was a pauperess when he died. I knew nothing—then—about the cost of living. None of our friends wanted to know me, so when the squire offered to help his dear friend's widow and child…I believed him. It seemed all perfectly above board." She shrugged. "I was stupid."

"A little naïve, perhaps," he corrected her, his gaze intense.

"Stupid," she repeated in a flat voice. "He said he'd keep an eye on me." She shuddered. "I didn't realise exactly what he meant by that."

"And that's why you feared for Amy that day when you left her with me. You thought you'd been 'stupid' again. Trusted another wrong 'un."

She nodded. They fell silent. It was too silent, she suddenly realised. *"Amy!"* Had she been hurt in the scuffle? Ellie raced into the cottage.

Her daughter was squatting before the fire, earnestly stirring the porridge. "It nearly burned, Mama," she said, "an' it was too heavy to lift and you said I wasn't to touch the fire things, so I just kept stirring it. Was that right?" She gave them an odd, guilty look.

Relieved, Ellie hugged her daughter. "Yes, darling, it was very right. Mr. Bruin has saved us and you have saved our breakfast."

He chuckled. "Nonsense, you were both well on the way to saving yourselves. Princess, I never would have expected it of you!" His laughter died as Amy's gaze dropped in shame.

"It's wicked to bite people, isn't it, Mama?" she whispered.

"Oh, my darling," Ellie's eyes misted. "You're not

wicked at all. I thought you were very brave and clever to do what you did."

"You mean you're not vexed with me, Mama?"

"No, indeed."

"And it's all right to bite the squire again?"

Before Ellie could reply, she and Amy were swept into Mr. Bruin's arms and whirled around the room in a mad, impromptu waltz. "Yes, indeed, Princess," he said. "You may bite the nasty old squire as often as you want. And your mama may hit him with a poker. And then when my two little Amazons are finished with him, I will toss him out the door."

Laughing, he set them down, then knelt down and said, "Princess Amy, you are one of the bravest, cleverest young ladies I know. Not only did you bite the evil Squiredragon and rescue yourself, you saved the porridge from burning! I would fain be your knight."

The little girl laughed delightedly, seized a wooden spoon and tapped him lightly on each shoulder. "Arise, Sir Bruin!"

Ellie laughed, even as her eyes filled. His nonsense had transformed the ugly incident into a bold adventure. He understood children so well... Too well for a bachelor?

"Are knights and princesses interested in porridge?" She forced a light-hearted note.

"Oh, yes, indee—"

Rat-tat-tat!

Everyone froze for a moment as the knock echoed through the small cottage.

"The squire," whispered Amy. "He's come back to put us in prison!"

"Blast him for his impudence! I'll see to this!" He

strode to the door and flung it open. "What the devil do you—?"

He stopped. A small, spare, neatly dressed man stood at the door.

"Gawd be praised, Capt'n!" said the man, beaming up at him. "When your horse came home without you, we all thought you was dead! Only I know'd better. I told 'em you was a survivor."

There was a sudden silence in the small cottage. The stranger's words seemed to echo. Ellie wondered whether anyone else could hear her heart thudding the way she could.

It was over, then, their brief idyll. He had been found.

"Capt'n? What's the matter?" The small man frowned at the tall, silent man in the doorway and then glanced behind him, to where Ellie and Amy stood, watchful and apprehensive. His bright bird-like gaze ran over Ellie and the little girl and his eyes narrowed.

The man he called Capt'n finally spoke. "Since I gather you know who I am, you'd better come in out of the cold."

The small man's head snapped back at that. "Know who you are? Are you bammin' me, Capt'n? Course I know who you are!"

"Come in, then."

He ushered the stranger inside and closed the door. He turned and met Ellie's gaze briefly. She couldn't read his expression. He began to offer a chair, then stopped in mid-movement. It was as if he was suddenly unsure of anything, she thought. Ellie filled the gap.

"Please, have a seat," she said to the stranger. "We were about to break our fast. It is only porridge and some milk, but you are very welcome to join us."

The man didn't respond. He continued to stare at "the Capt'n" with a puzzled expression.

"It's all right, the porridge isn't burnt," a little voice assured him. "I stopped it from getting burnt, didn't I, Mama?"

It broke the ice. Ellie couldn't help but smile and the stranger glanced down at Amy, smiled and said to Ellie, "I thank you for the offer, ma'am—and little miss—but I ate earlier. I wouldn't mind a drink to whet me whistle, though."

Ellie grimaced. "I'm sorry. There is only milk or water."

"Adam's ale will do me nicely, ma'am."

As Ellie fetched him a cup of water she glanced surreptitiously at Mr. Bruin. He was standing stiff and silent, a frown on his face. His body was braced, as if for a blow.

"Eat your porridge while it's hot," she said quietly. He sat down at the table and began to spoon porridge into his mouth.

They ate in silence, unanswered questions hovering over them, like the spectre at the feast. Even Amy was silent and anxious. The stranger watched the tableau, his eyes narrowed, going from one to the other, taking in everything.

Finally the porridge was finished, though Ellie doubted if anyone had enjoyed it. She began to collect the bowls, but Mr. Bruin stopped her with a gesture. He was nervous, Ellie knew. She sat down beside him again and took his hand.

The stranger noticed. She felt his disapproval and a sliver of ice slipped into her heart. It meant something, that look. It meant he thought she had no right to be holding this man's hand, this dear, battered hand, beloved in such a short time. He knew who her Mr. Bruin truly was. She hung on to the hand tighter, knowing it might be the last time.

She felt him squeeze her hard in response. He was as worried as she was. Amy came around the table and leaned against him. He put an arm around the little girl. Ellie felt a half-hysterical bubble of emotion rise in her throat. It was as if the three of them were a family, ranged defensively against the stranger, when, in fact, the opposite was true. This small spare man had come to take their beloved Mr. Bruin back to his true family.

"So, you say you know me. Then who am I?"

The stranger stared disbelievingly back at him.

Ellie explained in a flat voice, "He arrived here having been robbed and injured. His head was bleeding profusely and he slept like the dead for a night and a day. When he awoke, he had no recollection of anything—who he was, where he lived—nothing."

"Head injury, eh? That explains a lot."

At Ellie's look, he explained, "I've seen it before ma'am, in the army. Man gets hit on the head and loses it all for a time. Knew one bloke what never recovered all the memories, but most of 'em does." He turned. "You'll be all right, Capt'n Ambrose. Soon as I get you home, it'll all come back to you."

"Captain Ambrose? It doesn't sound the least bit familiar. What is my full name?"

"Capt'n Daniel Matthew Bramford Ambrose, late of the 5th Regiment."

Daniel. Ellie thought. It suited him.

"And you are?" said Daniel.

The small man leapt to his feet and saluted. "Sergeant

William Aloysius Tomkins, sir!" He waited a moment, then shrugged and sat down again. "Thought it might bring something back, sir. I was your sergeant for nigh on seven years. You call me Tomkins when you're with the nobs and Tommy when we're on our own."

Daniel smiled faintly. "So, I am…I was a soldier…"

The sergeant grinned. "Indeed you was, Capt'n, for the last seven years—all but a month or two—and a mighty good one, at that. Best man in a scrap anyone could ask for."

Daniel glanced down at his big battle-scarred hands and glanced up at Ellie, a rueful look in his eyes. She thought he'd been a fighter and he was, just not the sort of fighter she'd imagined. He wasn't a gutter brawler—he was possibly a hero.

Ellie found herself fighting a battle between wanting to hear more about him—and wanting to know nothing more, for with every word the sergeant spoke, her Mr. Bruin and the fragile dreams she'd built around him drifted further away from her…

"Where do I live?"

"Until recently, all over the Peninsula, fighting Boney, sir, but when your brother died a few months back, you sold out and came home. To Rothbury. Ring a bell, sir?"

Ellie knew it. It was a town about a half-day's travel to the north-west of her.

Daniel shook his head.

"No? Oh, well, it'll come, don't you worry." The sergeant paused, then said deliberately, "You have family responsibilities at Rothbury, Capt'n."

Family responsibilities. Ellie felt the sliver of ice slide deeper in her heart.

"Family responsibilities?" Daniel said at last. He was

squeezing Ellie's hand so tightly it was painful, but she couldn't bear to have him let go of her. It would happen all too soon.

"I have a wife, then?"

Say no, say no, say no! Ellie prayed silently. She could not breathe.

The stranger took an age to answer. He glanced at Ellie, then at Amy and then back at Daniel. And then said in the most ordinary of voices, "Yes, Capt'n, of course you have a wife. And a fine, beautiful lady she is, too."

Ellie could not breathe. Something was blocking her throat. *Of course he had a wife.* She had known it from the start. Stupid, stupid Ellie, to have let herself fall in love in a matter of days with a mysterious stranger.

He was strong and rugged and handsome, he was honourable, he was protective of women, he loved children. Of course he had a wife. He was altogether lovable.

And of course, his wife would be a fine, beautiful lady and probably sweet-natured and intelligent as well. She certainly wouldn't be a poverty-stricken, shabbily dressed widow. Stupid, stupid Ellie, thinking she had found love at last. Foolish, woolly-headed widgeon for forgetting that even when she had been a carefree young lady, passably pretty and very well dressed, she hadn't found love. She had needed her late father's money to buy her a husband. And not a very good one at that.

She'd long ago learned that fate was not her friend. She'd just forgotten the lesson.

The sergeant continued, "And, of course, your, um… Mrs. Ambrose has been terribly distressed by your disappearance."

Daniel nodded vaguely. He was still gripping her hand

so hard Ellie knew it would come up in a bruise later. Even so, she hung on to his hand for all she was worth. If a bruise was all she was going to have of him, then a bruise was what she would have. She could take that to bed with her instead. That and her dreams and memories. And regrets.

Regrets.

How she wished he hadn't been such a gentleman this morning.

"Mr. Bruin, you're squeezin' me too hard," complained Amy.

"Sorry, Princess," he murmured and gave her a gentle hug. "You run and play with your dolls while your mother and I talk to Sergeant Tomkins, here."

"I can't. The squire smashed them up and kicked them in the fire." Amy touched him, hesitantly. "Are you going to leave Mama and me, Mr. Bruin?" Her voice quavered.

That was Ellie's signal. Amy needed her mother to be strong. She wasn't going to fall apart. She wasn't going to be ruled by her instincts, those instincts which shrieked inside her to weep and cling and rage at fate, the instincts which had made her fall in love with a married man. He wasn't her Mr. Bruin; he was a Mr. Daniel Ambrose, with a loving wife awaiting his return. She had pride. She had her daughter to think of. She refused to disgrace herself.

Ellie wrenched her hand out of Daniel's, jumped to her feet and said brightly. "Yes, darling, isn't that wonderful for Mr. Bruin? Although he isn't Mr. Bruin any more, he's Mr. Ambrose. And Sergeant Tomkins is his friend and has come to take him home to his family, who is waiting for him and who love him very much and miss him terribly. Isn't that exciting? Now come and help Mama wash these dishes and let the gentlemen talk." She gathered up the bowls, knowing she was babbling, smiling so hard she thought her face would split.

But Amy didn't move. She fixed big blue eyes on Daniel and asked in a tragic little voice, "Have you already got a little girl of your own, Mr. Bruin?"

He stroked her curly head with a big, gentle hand. His voice was deep and husky and it seemed to catch in his throat as he said, "I don't know, Princess. Have I got a little girl, Sergeant? Or any children at all?"

The sergeant tugged at the neatly tied stock around his stiff collar. He cleared his throat. "Er…not yet, sir. Though…er, hrrumph, your mother has…er, expectations of…of being made a grandmother…soon. She speaks of it often."

Oh mercy, his wife must be expecting a child. Ellie closed her eyes and swished the bowls and water frantically, appearing busy. "Oh! So you are anticipating a happy event! How splendid! No wonder your wife is so anxious about you, Mr. Ambrose. A woman is always more emotional at that…delicate time. What delightful anticipation for your mother. To be a grandmother must be marvellous. A child has a special relationship with a grandmother. If she has one, that is. Amy never had a grandmother. They both died before she was born."

Foolish, babbling Ellie. She forced herself to take a deep breath and added brightly, "It's so amazingly lucky that Sergeant Tomkins managed to find you in such an out-of-the-way place. How did you find him, Sergeant? Tell us the whole story."

The sergeant regarded her thoughtfully for a moment and then explained to Daniel, "You'd decided to go to Newcastle to order some new clothes, them that you'd come home from the wars with bein' unfit for company, so your mother said, an' nothing in the house to fit you, your late brother bein' a smaller man than you, sir."

That explained the worn and shabby clothes, thought Ellie sadly as she rubbed apathetically at the dishes. They'd been to war with him.

"You'd decided to stay for a few weeks, to get out of your m—" The sergeant stopped and cleared his throat. "You were feeling a little restless at Rothbury, sir. So you sent me on ahead to find lodgings and set up a few appointments. But when you didn't arrive in the lodgings I got worried—you being a man what keeps to your word, sir."

Oh, yes, he kept to his word, thought Ellie regretfully, thinking of those few glorious moments when she'd woken in his arms. And he'd told her to go. On his honour.

"So then when they sent word that your horse had been found but no sign of you, I came a'lookin'. I asked in every village between here and town, lookin' in every ditch and gully and clump of trees, headin' for Rothbury. And then I saw a pair of boots, sir, on sale in the market place, and I thinks to myself, I've seen them boots before."

There was a pause and the sergeant said a little throatily. "I don't mind saying the sight of them boots gave me a right nasty turn, Capt'n, because I figured the only way you'd give up your boots was if you was dead."

He loved Daniel, too, thought Ellie sadly. And he'd grieved when he thought him dead.

"So then I went to the church, to see if the minister had buried anyone lately. He told me you were alive and in the care of a local widow…" He glanced at Ellie and then back at Daniel. "I bought back your boots. And there's a change of clothes for you, sir, in the bag there."

An awkward silence fell in the cottage.

"Ah, right," Daniel finally said. "Good thinking, Sergeant."

Ellie forced herself to say it. To get it over with. "So, Mr. Daniel Ambrose, you'd better put on your boots and change your clothes. With any luck this mild weather will hold and you will be home to your wife by this evening." She smiled, a wide, desperate smile that stretched her lips and made her jaw ache. Could a smile shatter a person? She hoped not.

"Oh, Ellie," he said softly and put out a hand.

She wanted to grab it, to cling and never let him go, but she turned away instead. "Hurry up, then." She felt her eyes fill and blinked furiously to keep them from spilling down her cheeks. "You don't want to keep the sergeant waiting. Your wi—" Her voice cracked. "Your family is waiting to hear the news that you are alive."

Daniel watched her turn away. He felt ill. *He had a wife!* Dammit! How could he have forgotten that? The sergeant seemed to think this wife loved him, too. Had he loved her, this unknown beautiful lady who was expecting his child?

And if he had, how could he go on loving her, now that he had found Ellie?

Because he didn't believe it was possible to love anyone more than he loved Ellie. He might not remember any details of his life, but right at this moment he knew, deep within himself, in his bones and his blood, that he loved Ellie with every shred of his being.

Had he loved another woman in this same way, with this

intensity of feeling, before he was hit on the head by footpads?

This wife meant nothing to him now. Would Ellie mean nothing to him once his memory was regained? The thought terrified him. He didn't want his memories. He wanted Ellie.

He looked at her. She turned away, her mouth stretched in a travesty of a smile, her eyes brimming with tears. She was trying so hard to be brave and cheerful, not to make him feel bad. Oh Ellie, Ellie… How was it possible to love someone so much in such a short time? How was it possible to lose so much with one blow?

And how was he ever going to leave her?

The sergeant handed him his boots.

Ellie watched Daniel trudge up the stairs to her bedroom for the last time. Her hands were busy wiping the table down, but her mind was with him, imagining every move he made. The way he pulled off his shirt, the look and feel of the broad, hard chest underneath, his beautiful sculpted shoulders, the way he bent his head when— "Here y'are, Mrs. Carmichael. This should cover everything."

Ellie blinked. The sergeant was holding something out to her. Without thinking she extended her hand and took it. Then she glanced down. It was a small leather pouch. It was heavy and the contents clinked. "What is this?"

"Payment."

"Payment? For what?"

"For looking after Capt'n Ambrose, of course. What else?"

It was as if he had slapped her. She gathered her

dignity together and laid the pouch gently on the table. "No, thank you."

The sergeant frowned. "Ain't it enough?"

Ellie stared at the man incredulously. Her heart was breaking and he thought she wanted to haggle over a few coins? "No payment is necessary, Sergeant."

The sergeant jutted his chin mulishly. "Capt'n Ambrose always pays his shot."

Ellie just looked at him. He shifted, uneasy under her gaze.

"Ellie, could you help me with this for a moment?" Daniel called from upstairs.

"Coming," she called. "Put your money away, Sergeant Tomkins," she said wearily. "It's not wanted here."

The moment she entered the upstairs room he pulled her into his arms. He hugged her hard against his body and she could feel his need and his pain. "I don't want to leave you," he groaned and covered her mouth with his, tasting her hungrily, devouring her.

It was nothing like the gentle, teasing, warmly passionate kisses of the morning. This was need, pure and simple. Heat. Desperation. Fear and desire. Urgency.

Ellie returned every kiss, each caress in equal urgency, knowing she might never see him again. Oh, why had they not made love this morning? Her foolish scruples seemed meaningless, now she was faced with the probability of a life without Daniel.

She shook with the force of the knowledge.

He took her head in his hands, his palms framing her face. His eyes burned into her soul. "Ellie, I *promise* you, this isn't the end. I'll sort something out." His voice was ragged. "I'll try to come back and see—"

Ellie shook her head. "No, Daniel. It must be a clean break. I could not bear to live on crumbs." She kissed him fiercely. "I want all of you. Crumbs would be the worst form of torture. As it is, I will have my memories. Only I wish we had…you know…this morning."

"Made love," he corrected her, in a low, husky voice. "Not *you know*. You mean you wish we had made love."

Tears spilled down her cheeks and she said in a broken voice, "No, Daniel, even without the…the consummation, we have already made…created love. Can you not feel it all around us? I hope we made enough, for it's going to have to last me the rest of my life…"

"Oh, Ellie, my sweet, lovely Ellie." He groaned and held her tighter, "How can I bear to leave you?"

"You must, Daniel. You have a wife. There is no choice for either of us."

"Ready, Capt'n?" called the sergeant from downstairs. "Need a hand with anything?"

"Blast him," muttered Daniel. He clung to her, burying his face in her hair, inhaling the scent of her, the scent of life, of love. He wished they had celebrated their love physically, for it would add a dimension he thought she was unaware of. But she was right; even without that consummation, they had already created so much love.

He desperately hoped it was enough to survive the return of his memories.

Finally, reluctantly, they pulled apart and went downstairs. Ellie felt the sergeant's shrewd gaze run over her, and knew that she looked like a woman who had just kissed and been well kissed in return. She raised her chin. She did not care what he thought of her.

The sergeant had brought two horses. They were saddled. Ready. Waiting.

"What about the squire?" said Daniel in a rough under-voice. "I canno—"

Ellie put her hands over his lips. "Hush. Don't worry about it. I've been dealing with him for months. Nothing has changed." His mouth twisted under her fingers. He touched them with his tongue and she pulled them away, unable to take much more.

"Mr. Bruin, Mr. Bruin, you're not goin', are you?"

Daniel picked up the distressed little girl and hugged her. "I have to, Princess. Now, be a good girl and look after your mother for me, won't you?" He kissed her goodbye.

Amy wept and clung to his neck. "No, no, Mr. Bruin, you have to stay. The wishing candle brought you…"

His face rigid with the effort of staying in control, Daniel unhooked the small, desperate hands and passed Amy over to her mother.

"I *will* sort something out, I promise you," he said in a low, ragged voice.

"Don't make promises you cannot keep."

"I always keep my promises. Always." His eyes were damp. They clung to her, but he didn't kiss or touch Ellie again. She was relieved. Neither of them could have borne it.

The best way to perform drastic surgery was fast. He turned and strode to the horses, mounting his in one fluid movement. He turned in the saddle, looked across the clearing at Ellie and her daughter with burning blue eyes and said, *"Always."* And he galloped away.

Always, thought Ellie miserably. Did he mean he always kept his promises? Or that he would always love her? Whichever it was, it didn't matter. He was gone. She had the rest of the day to get through somehow, a sunset to await, a daughter to feed and tuck into bed and watch over until she fell asleep. Only then could she seek her own bed and find the release she needed.

The release she needed. Tears and sleep. Not the release she craved...

She carried Amy into the cottage. Making a drink for them both, she found the small pouch of money the sergeant had offered her hidden away behind the milk jug. She looked inside it. Twenty pounds. A fortune, enough to keep her and Amy fed for a long time yet.

Capt'n Ambrose always pays his shot. The sergeant had prevailed yet again.

Somehow, she got through the rest of the day.

When it came time to go up to bed, Amy trotted ahead of her mother, up the stairs.

"Mama." Amy turned, her freshly washed little face lit up. "Look what I found on my bed." She held up a tiny wooden doll, carved, a little clumsily, out of birchwood. "It's got blue eyes, just like me. An' Mr. Bruin, too." Amy's eyes shone.

A thick lump formed in Ellie's throat. Daniel's whittling. She'd thought he'd been simply killing time, making wood shavings, but he'd made her daughter a doll.

"It's lovely, darling. I'll make her some clothes tomorrow."

"Not her. This is a boy doll," said Amy firmly. "I'll call him Daniel, after Mr. Bruin."

"L...lovely." Ellie managed a smile, though she feared it wobbled a bit.

* * *

Later, when Amy was asleep, and the cold descended around her so that she could delay the moment no more, Ellie stepped reluctantly into her own room. Her eyes were drawn inevitably to the sleeping alcove, to the bed.

And then, finally, the tears came, for of course there was nothing there. Not even a small wooden doll. There was never going to be a Daniel there for her again.

He was gone.

Chapter Four

"No, darling, I cannot make you a new dolls' house yet. Not until we find a new house of our own. Houses for people come before houses for dolls."

Amy nodded. "The squire doesn't like us any more, does he, Mama?"

"No, darling he doesn't. Now help Mama pack by bringing all your clothes down here. I'm going to bundle them all up in a sheet, so we can put them on Ned's cart."

"Don't worry, Mama. If the squire comes back again, Daniel will hit him for us again, won't you Daniel?" Amy gestured fiercely with her small wooden Daniel.

"Nobody is hitting anybody," snapped Ellie. "Now fetch your things down here at once."

Ellie bit her lip as, chastened, Amy did her bidding. She had no idea where they were going to live. The vicar had offered them a room in the vicarage until after Christmas, but then his pupils would return for their lessons and there would be no room. But she was sure she would find something soon.

She had to.

Rat-tat-tat!

She froze. The squire had been back twice already since Daniel had left. Ellie remembered her daughter's words and her temper suddenly flared. She didn't need a Daniel to protect her; a wooden Daniel would do no good and the real Daniel...well, the real Daniel was back where he belonged, with his loving wife who was expecting their child. Daniel would be there to protect that woman and that child, not the woman and child he had stumbled across in a storm, brought by the light of a gypsy candle.

His memory would no doubt have returned by now. He probably didn't even remember Ellie. Whereas, she...she remembered everything. Too much, in fact. She couldn't forget a thing. He was there, in her mind and her heart, every time she slipped into a cold and empty bed. And she woke with the thought of Daniel every morning, missing his warm caresses, the low rumble of his voice... Bitter regret choked her as she recalled how she had fended him off. If only they had made love...just once.

It wasn't only in bed that he haunted her. He was there, in every corner of her cottage, in the stories her daughter prattled, in the doll he'd made for her. Ellie stoked the fire, morning, noon and night, with wood that Daniel had chopped, and her mouth still dried as she remembered the way his shoulder muscles bunched and flowed with each fall of the axe.

He was there each time it rained and her roof didn't leak. Her heart still caught in her throat when she recalled the way he'd come down off the roof in such a rush, giving her such a fright. The moment she realised she loved him...

It had rained most days since Daniel had left.

The knocker banged again. Ellie forced the bitter lump from her throat. She lifted the poker, strode to the door and flung it open, weapon brandished belligerently.

There was no one there. The rain had stopped and a heavy mist had fallen. It swirled and ebbed, making the cottage surroundings eerily fluid. Poker held high, Ellie stepped out on to the wet ground.

"Hello, Ellie." The deep voice seeped into her frozen bones like heat.

She whirled around, stared, could say nothing. The fog eddied around a tall silhouette, wrapped in a dark cloak, but the cloak was no disguise to Ellie. She knew every plane of that body, had been living with it in her mind and her heart for weeks.

"What are you doing here, Daniel?" she managed to croak.

He moved towards her. "I've come for you, Ellie. I want you with me."

Pain streaked through Ellie. The words she had so wanted, but now it was all wrong. She held up the poker, as if to ward him off, and shook her head. "No, Daniel. I can't. I won't. I have Amy to think of."

He stood stock-still, shocked, his brow furrowed. "But of course I want Amy as well."

Ellie shook her head, more frantically. "No, I can't do that. I won't. Go back home, Daniel. No matter what my feelings for you are, I won't come with you. I won't ruin Amy's life that way."

There was a long silence. Behind her Ellie could hear the slow plop, plop of water dripping off the roof…the roof he had fixed for her.

"And what *are* your feelings for me?"

Ellie's face crumpled with anguish. "You know what they are," she whispered.

He shook his head. His eyes blazed with intensity. "No, I thought I did, but now…I'm only sure of my own feelings." He took a deep breath and said in a voice vibrating with emotion, "I love you, Ellie. I have my memory back and I know I have never loved anyone and will never love anyone again as much as I love you. You are my heart, Ellie."

Tears blurred Ellie's vision at his words. All she'd ever dreamed of was in those few words… *You are my heart, Ellie.* But it was too late.

"Go back to your wife, Daniel," she said miserably and turned away.

There was a short, fraught silence. Then Daniel swore. Then he laughed. "I'd forgotten that."

Ellie turned. "Forgotten your wife?" she said, shocked.

Daniel's blue eyes blazed into her. "I don't have a wife. I've never had a wife. It was all a stupid misunderstanding." He laid his hand over his heart and declared, "I am a single man, in possession of all my wits and I'm able to support a wife in relative comfort. I love you most desperately, Mrs. Ellie Carmichael, and I've come to ask you to be my wife."

There was a long silence. Ellie just stared. The raised poker wavered. A strong masculine hand took it gently out of her slackened grasp.

"Well, Ellie-love, aren't you going to answer me?"

Ellie couldn't see him for tears, but she could feel him and she flung herself into his arms and kissed him fiercely. "Oh, Daniel, Daniel, yes, of course I'll marry you! I love you so much it hurts!"

* * *

"The sergeant lied," Daniel explained some time later, an arm around both Ellie and Amy. "The silly clunch thought he was rescuing me from a designing hussy. He'd started to wonder if he'd made a mistake—apparently you just about gave him frostbite when he offered you money—but he thought it would be better to get me out of your clutches and recover my memory before I made any decisions."

He grinned and kissed Ellie again. "So, having regained my memory, I've brought myself straight back to your clutches. And what very nice clutches they are, too, my dear," he leered in a growly voice and both Ellie and Amy giggled.

"So you remember everything, now?"

"Indeed I do. The moment I arrived back at Rothbury, it all came back to me. Most peculiar how the mind works—or doesn't, as the case may be. Rothbury is a house as well as a village," he explained. "I was born there."

"And, er, what do you do there?" Ellie enquired delicately.

"I oversee the farm. I've found a position for you, too. You will be in charge of the house. After we're married, of course." He looked at her. "You're sure, Ellie? Knowing nothing about me, you'll marry me and come and keep house with me?"

She smiled mistily and nodded happily. "Oh, yes, please. I could think of nothing more wonderful. I would be a good housekeeper, I think. In fact, I did try to find a position like that after Hart died and we found there was no money left, but having no references…and also a daughter…" She hesitated. "You know I bring nothing to this marriage."

He looked affronted. "You bring yourself, don't you? You're all I want, love. Just you. Oh, and a small bonus called Princess Amy."

"Oh, Daniel…" She kissed him again. It was that or weep all over him.

He had brought a special licence. "I've arranged everything, my love. The vicar has agreed to marry us this afternoon—no need to wait for the banns to be called. Then Tommy—Sergeant Tomkins to you—will take Amy to stay the night at the vicarage."

"But why—"

He looked at her and his blue eyes were suddenly burning with intensity. "We have a wedding night ahead of us, love…and this is a small cottage. Amy is better off at the vicarage. Don't worry, she already has Tommy eating out of her hand. He loves a bossy woman! And the vicar is delighted, too. He loves Christmas weddings."

Christmas. They were only a few days away from Christmas. She'd been trying to forget about it, expecting this to be her worst Christmas ever. But now…

Daniel continued, "We'll stay one night here and then I'll take you home to Rothbury. I thought it would be nice if we celebrated Christmas there, with my poor old mother."

Ellie smiled. "Oh, yes, that would be lovely. But…a wedding, today…I have noth—" She glanced down at the shabby dress she wore. "I don't suppose my old blue dress—"

"You look beautiful in anything, my love, but I brought you a dress…and some other things." He gestured to a portmanteau, which the sergeant had carried in earlier.

Hesitantly Ellie opened the lid. Inside, wrapped in tissue, was a beautiful heavy cream satin dress. She lifted it out and held it against herself. The dress was exquisite, long-sleeved and high-waisted, embroidered over the bodice and around the hem in the most delicate and lovely green-and-gold silk embroidery. It was utterly beautiful… Totally unsuitable for a housekeeper, of course, but did she care?

"Is it all right?"

She turned, clutching the dress to her breasts and whispered, "It's beautiful, Daniel."

"The colour is all right, is it?"

She smiled. "It's lovely, though I'm not exactly a maiden, Daniel."

"You are to me," he said. "Anyway, that wasn't why I chose it. It reminded me of when I first saw you—you were dressed in that white night-thingummy."

Ellie thought of her much-patched, thick flannel night-gown and laughed. "Only a man could see any similarity between my shapeless old nightgown and this beautiful thing." She laid the dress carefully over the chair and flew across the room to hug and kiss him.

"A man in love," he corrected her. "And that night-gown did have shape—your shape, and a delectable shape it is too." He ran his hands over her lovingly and kissed her deeply. Ellie kissed him back, shivering with pleasurable anticipation.

"Enough of that, my love. We'll be churched before long. We can wait until tonight."

"I don't know if I can," she whispered.

He laughed, lifted her in his arms and swung her around exuberantly, then kissed her again and pushed her towards the table. "There's more stuff in the portmanteau."

She looked and drew out a lovely green merino pelisse, trimmed with white fur at the collar and cuffs and a pair of pretty white boots which even looked to be the right size. Beneath it was a miniature pelisse identical to the first, but in blue. With it was a dainty little blue dress with a charming lace collar. And the sweetest pair of tiny fur-lined red kid boots, perfect winter wear for a little girl. Ellie's eyes misted. He'd brought a wedding outfit for Amy, too. And of the finest quality. She wondered how he could afford it, but it didn't matter.

She smiled a wobbly smile and hugged him. How did she ever deserve such a dear, kind thoughtful man? "Thank you, Daniel. I don't know how—"

"Come on, love, let's get you to that church, or we'll be anticipating our vows. The sergeant shall escort you and Amy. I shall meet you there, as is proper." He pulled out a fob-watch and consulted it. "Shall we say one hour?"

"One hour!" gasped Ellie. "Two, at least. Amy and I need to wash our hair and—"

"Very well, two hours it is," he said briskly and kissed her mouth, a swift, hard, possessive promise of a kiss. "And not a moment longer, mind! I have waited long enough!"

Freshly prepared for Christmas, the church looked beautiful. Small and built of sombre grey stone, it glowed inside as the soft winter sunshine pierced the stained-glass windows, flooding the inside with rainbows of delicate colour and making the brass and silver gleam. It smelt of beeswax and fresh-cut pinewood. Greenery decorated the softly shining oak pews and the two huge brass urns on either side of the altar were laden with branches of holly and ivy and pine. Braziers had been lit, taking the chill from the air, throwing out a cosy glow.

Ellie and Amy, dressed in their new finery, stood at the door. The sergeant, looking smart and neat in what Ellie guessed was a new coat, had gone to inform Daniel and the vicar of their arrival. Ellie, suddenly nervous, clutched Amy's hand. Was she doing the right thing? She had only known Daniel a matter of days, after all.

She loved him. But she had loved once before…and had been badly mistaken. She had never felt for Hart half the feelings she had for Daniel. Did that mean she had made the right choice this time…or double the mistake? She shivered, feeling suddenly cold. Amy's little hand was warm in hers. A tiny white fur muff dangled from her daughter's wrist. A gift from Daniel…

"Are you ready, love?" The deep voice came from her right. Ellie jumped. Daniel was standing there, with a look in his eyes that drove all the last-minute jitters from her mind.

"Oh, yes. I'm ready," she said, and with a full heart laid her hand on his arm.

"Then lead the way, Sergeant and Amy."

Gravely the sergeant offered his arm to the small girl. Like a little princess, Amy walked solemnly beside him down the aisle. As they reached the altar, Amy's attention was distracted. "Look, Mama, the vicar has a dolls' house, too," she whispered.

Ellie followed her daughter's gesture and her hand tightened on Daniel's arm. To the right of the aisle at the front of the church sat a Christmas diorama on a small wooden table. A stable, thatched with straw, was surrounded by carved wooden sheep and cows and a donkey.

Over the building a painted wooden star gleamed. Inside the stable stood a woman in a blue painted robe, a woman with a serene expression and kind eyes. Beside her stood a tall dark-haired man smiling down at a child not his own, with love in his eyes and his heart.

Like the man at Ellie's side.

Amy stared at the diorama in fascination. She was too small to remember it from the previous Christmas. "The vicar's dolls' house has a family, too—a mama and a papa and a baby, just like us, only I'm not a baby any more."

Ellie glanced up at the tall man by her side, looking at Amy as if he'd just received the most wonderful of gifts. She said huskily, "That's right, darling. It's a very special family. That's Mary and that's Joseph and that's little Baby Jesus."

"It's lovely." Amy was entranced.

Daniel's arm tightened around Ellie and he drew her forward as the vicar began.

"Dearly beloved…"

Daniel and Ellie returned to the cottage alone, their footsteps crunching on the cold ground, anticipation their only companion. Daniel lit a fire downstairs, then went upstairs to light another one in the bedroom, while Ellie laid out some supper. They ate almost in silence, eating slowly, barely touching the wine and the game pie that Daniel had brought.

He laid down his knife and fork and said with a wry smile, "I can't think of a word to say or take in a mouthful of food, love, for wanting you. Shall we go upstairs?"

Tremulously she nodded.

They walked up the stairs with arms wrapped tight

around each other. Ellie recalled that first frightful battle to get him up the stairs, his dogged courage as he took each step, and felt a fresh surge of love. How far they had come in such a short time…

When they reached the bedroom, she hesitated, suddenly realising she should have gone up ahead of him and changed into her nightgown. She glanced at the curtains across the sleeping alcove and wondered if she should go behind them to change. It would be a little awkward. There was not much room.

She glanced up at Daniel and the questions in her mind dissipated like smoke as his mouth came down over hers in a tender kiss. She leaned into him, returning the kiss with all her heart. Her hands curled into his hair, loving the feel of hard bone beneath crisp short waves. She could feel the place where he had been injured, where she had cut his hair away.

Daniel felt her trembling against him. He wanted her so much, wanted to dive on to the bed with her and make her his in one bold passionate glorious movement. She was his! His beloved. The woman of his heart. Ellie. Pressing small moist kisses over his face. So soft, so warm, so giving. He felt proud, primitive, possessive.

But she was trembling. And it was not simply desire.

He recalled her shock when he'd touched her intimately, all those mornings ago, her surprise and bemusement at the pleasure his hands had given her. He deepened the kiss, feeling a jolt like lightning surge through him at her enthusiastic, yet endearingly inexpert return of his caresses. She was a married woman, a mother, and a widow, his little Ellie, but of the pleasures between a man and woman she seemed almost as ignorant as any new bride.

Daniel reined in his desires and set himself to introduce his love to the joys between a man and woman. He rained her soft, smooth skin with kisses, running his hands over her, soothing her anxieties wordlessly, caressing her, warming, knowing her.

The cream of the silk gown looked heavy and lifeless against the vibrant delicacy of Ellie's skin. He unbuttoned the gown, pearl button by pearl button, revealing more and more of her soft, silken skin. He slipped the gown off her shoulders and she flushed shyly under his gaze, all the way down to her pink-tipped breasts. It was the most beautiful flush he had ever seen. He bent to kiss her and when his mouth closed over one nipple she arched against him, crying out with a small muffled groan and clasping his head to her breast.

He glanced up at her and his body pounded with heat and need as he saw her head flung back, her eyes blind with passion. Mastering his own needs, he moved his attention to her other breast, and was rewarded by a long shuddery moan.

Daniel slowly divested her of her clothing, piece by piece, for once not feeling impatient with the quantity and complexity of the underclothes women wore, because as he slid each garment over her skin, she blushed most deliciously and shuddered sensually under the warmth of his hands as they pushed the soft cotton slowly over her skin. He hazily made a note to get her silk underclothes. A few minutes later he changed his mind. It would be better if she wore no underclothes at all…

Finally she was naked, soft and peachy in the flames of the fire he had built. Blushing, she glanced at the bed-clothes and then back at him and he realised she would want to cover herself while he disrobed. She was shy and modest, his little Ellie.

She surprised him. "My turn, I think." Eager hands made short work of his neckcloth and shirt buttons. She hesitated when it came to the fastenings of his breeches, then reached for him. He gritted his teeth, fighting for control as she fumbled with the buttons, frowning with concentration, her hands brushing against his arousal, her breasts swaying softly.

She unfastened the breeches and slowly pushed them down his legs. And stared. It was almost as if she had never seen a naked man before, the way she stared, enthralled. And then she reached out and touched him and he could hold back no longer. He tumbled her back on the bed, and, with none of the finesse he prided himself on, entered her in one long powerful thrust. She was hot and moist and ready for him and she arched against him, her body pulling him in, closing in, welcoming him…and as his body claimed her, totally out of his control, she stiffened, her eyes suddenly wide with shock.

"Daniel," she panted. "What is happen—?" She arched all around him and her body began to shudder uncontrollably.

"Let yourself go, love. I am here," he gritted out, himself on the brink of climax.

"Oh, Daniel, Daniel. I love you!" And she shattered around him, sending him over the edge of bliss into oblivion…

He had never known it could be like that. Daniel gazed at his beautiful, rumpled sleeping new bride with bemused wonder. He had thought he would be the one to initiate Ellie into a new world of lovemaking between a man and woman. But if he had shown her a new world, she had shown him one too, a world he'd never even dreamed existed. The world of making love with the woman you adored. Physical pleasures, he'd realised, were shallow ephemeral moments, compared with how it had been with Ellie. The moment when she'd come to climax—her first ever...

Would he, could he, ever forget that look in her eyes as she gazed into his, shouting that she loved him...as she shattered with pleasure, sending him into oblivion with her?

It was like looking at a painting all your life and not knowing there was a living breathing whole new dimension waiting on the other side of the canvas. Like eating all your life and not knowing there was such a thing as salt...

No, there were no poetical images to describe making love with Ellie. All Daniel knew was that he wanted to live to a very ripe old age so he could love her every day of his life.

He leaned down and began to wake her with his mouth, smiling as she squirmed with sleepy pleasure, reaching for him even before she was awake...

At mid-morning, a coach arrived to take them to Rothbury. It bore a crest on the side panel. Ellie glanced at Daniel in surprise. It seemed rather a grand coach for a farmer.

He grinned at her. "It belongs to the Dowager Viscountess, Lady Rothbury, my love. When I told her I was bringing a bride to Rothbury, she insisted I use her carriage."

"She must be a very kind-hearted lady."

"You might say that," agreed Daniel wryly. "I put it down to a managing disposition, myself. The woman has made my life a misery since she lost her husband and her eldest son."

"Oh, the poor lady. She must be lonely, Daniel."

He nodded. "Yes, she has not enough to do. However, she is expecting her first grandchild any day now and I am hopeful that the child will keep her out of my hair in future." He picked up a bundle of Ellie's possessions and winked. "At any rate, having no conveyance of my own as yet, I wasn't about to look her gift-carriage in the mouth."

"I should think not." Ellie frowned thoughtfully as she hurried to collect her things. It was clear that Daniel was a little irritated by his employer's managing ways. She hoped she could smooth the way between them.

Because of their imminent eviction, Ellie was already packed. She left her chickens for Ned to take, as Daniel said he already had plenty. There was nothing else. In a few minutes, their meagre possessions were placed in the boot of the coach and they'd picked up Amy and the sergeant and were heading north.

The trip to Rothbury was long, but not tedious. They passed the time with songs and games for Amy's entertainment. And with small secret glances and touches, which recalled in Ellie the magic and the splendour of her wedding night and morning and raised in her body the shivery, delightful expectation of nights and mornings yet to come.

Ellie thought of how she had told Daniel weeks before that they had already "made love," without having joined, flesh with flesh. She remembered the look on his face as she'd said it, a little quizzical, a little knowing…indulgent.

How naïve she'd been. She hadn't understood that the act of making love with Daniel would bring another dimension to that love, a deep, powerful intimacy that was not merely physical…though it was intensely physical. She would never forget that first, almost terrifying intimacy, the intensity as she'd exploded into helpless, splintering waves of pleasure under his eyes.

She'd assumed that because the physical act had been unimportant in her marriage to Hart, it would be the same with Daniel. She'd believed it was, by its nature, crude, furtive and only necessary for the procreation of an heir. Because that's how Hart had seen it.

But nothing was the same with Daniel. With Daniel it was…a joyous celebration. A glorious, elemental claiming, in which they united in a way that she had never imagined. It was not a mere fleshly joining—it was…everything. Body, mind, soul. She shivered with remembrance. And pleasure. With Daniel it had been an act of reverence as well as earthy delight. They had made love so many times and the echo of it was with her still. It was as if in one night their bodies had become forever joined, with invisible, unbreakable threads.

The coach swayed along. Awareness shimmered between them, recalling moments of shattering delight. She did not simply love Daniel, she was part of him. And he of her.

With tender eyes she watched him, playing a children's clapping game with Amy, pretending bearish clumsiness with his big, calloused hands. She felt a ripple, deep within her body, as she watched. There was nothing clumsy about those big, beautiful hands. They had taught her body how to sing; it was singing still, within her, deep and silent.

He had transformed her in the night, murmuring endearments, caressing her in places never before caressed, creating sensations she'd never known...nor even imagined. It was as if he knew her body better than she did herself.

Ellie caught his eye, and saw the lurking wolf-smile in it. His gaze sharpened, as if he knew what she'd been thinking, and she felt herself blush as his look turned suddenly intense and hungry. He wanted her. In the course of a single night he'd loved every part of her with hands and mouth and eyes, bringing her alive as she'd never known was possible. And she'd gloried in it so that the wonder still spilled from her...

She couldn't wait for the night to come. Last night she had been the novice, reduced to a blissful jelly by his loving attentions, but it hadn't escaped her that he seemed to enjoy being touched the same way she did. Tonight it would be her turn to explore him. She felt herself smile, a small, secret triumphant feminine smile, and then she caught his eye again, and blushed scarlet as if he'd read her mind.

Passion. She'd never understood it before. An incendiary mix of primitive power...and sublime pleasure. Explosive. Ready to reignite at a look, a touch, a thought...

Though it was only afternoon, dark was falling by the time they turned in at two large stone gateposts, topped by lions. They received their first sight of Rothbury House a few moments later.

It was ablaze with light. The house was huge with dozens of windows. In every window there were candles burning. As they drew closer, Ellie could see they were red candles. Christmas candles.

"Remember how you told me about your wishing candle?" Daniel addressed Amy. "Those are wishing candles for us, to bring us all home safe and sound."

Amy's eyes shone. Ellie lifted his hand and held it against her cheek. It wasn't true—it was probably a tradition of the Big House, but it was a lovely thought, to make a little girl feel welcomed. Daniel put his arm around Ellie and smiled.

The coach pulled up at a flight of steps. "The front door?" whispered Ellie, surprised.

Daniel shrugged. "I'm under orders to present you to the Dowager without delay. She prides herself on knowing everyone on the estate. And it is her carriage, don't forget."

"Oh, dear!" Ellie nervously ran a hand over her hair and tried to smooth her travel-crushed clothing. She hoped the Dowager would not be too demanding an employer.

In the magnificent hallway, an elegant lady awaited them. Silver-haired, she was the epitome of elegance, dressed in the first stare of fashion in a black gown, a black shawl in Norwich silk dangling negligently from her elbows.

"Ellie, I'd like you to meet the Dowager Viscountess, Lady Rothbury," said Daniel.

Ellie curtsied to her new employer.

"Mother, this is my wife, Elinor, the new Viscountess of Rothbury."

Ellie, still curtsying, nearly fell over. Daniel bent down and helped her up.

"But I thought I was to be the new housekeeper!" gasped Ellie. "You mean, you're, you're—"

He bowed. "Viscount Rothbury, at your service, my dear." His blue, blue eyes twinkled wickedly as he kissed her hand in a way that made Ellie blush.

"My son is tiresomely reticent about some things," the

lady said sympathetically. "He told *me* he was bringing home a cottage wench, but you are as beautiful and elegant as any of the suitable young ladies I have been flinging so uselessly at his head this age."

"Much more beautiful," growled Daniel's deep voice and he grinned down at Ellie, who looked flustered and adoring at the same time.

The Dowager Viscountess gave a small, satisfied nod. She moved forward and drew Ellie into a warm, scented embrace. "Welcome to the family, my dear girl. I think you will do very nicely indeed for my scapegrace son."

"The scapegrace son agrees with you, Mother."

Lady Rothbury's eyes dropped to where Amy was loitering in the shadows of her mother's skirts, a little overwhelmed by everything that had happened. "And who have we here?" she said softly. "Can this be my beautiful new granddaughter? My son promised me I would love her instantly."

Ellie's chest was suddenly tight. Such welcome as this she had never dared to dream of. Her daughter would be loved in this house.

Amy examined the older lady with wide, candid eyes. "Are you really Mr. Bruin's mama?"

"Mr. Bruin? Is that what you call my son? Yes, I am his mama. May I ask why you call him Mr. Bruin?"

"That's 'cause he looked just like a bear when he came to me and Mama. He was all prickly."

Lady Rothbury laughed. "A most perspicacious young lady. A prickly bear is exactly how I would describe my son at times." She smiled down at Amy.

Amy looked thoughtful. "I haven't got a grandmother," the little girl said shyly.

The Dowager Viscountess held out her hand and said softly, "You have one now." Amy glanced at her mother for permission, then, beaming, took the older lady's hand.

Lady Rothbury smiled at Ellie through tear-blurred eyes. "Thank you, my dear. You have made my son and me happier than I would have believed possible."

Ellie couldn't say a word. She was blinking away her own tears.

"Now," continued the older lady, "I have something for my beautiful new granddaughter—a welcome home present which I hope she will enjoy. It isn't new, I'm afraid—it was mine when I was a little girl. I kept it for my daughters, but I was never blessed with any, so it has remained untouched in the attic these many years. When Daniel told me about his Ellie and her Amy, I had it brought down and cleaned up and I must say, it looks almost as good as it did when I was a child."

Ellie looked quizzically at Daniel. He shrugged and murmured, "No idea."

"Come along, Amy." The little girl's hand held fast in hers, Lady Rothbury swept down the hall.

Grinning, Daniel called, "She's a princess, Mother. You have to call her Princess Amy."

His mother turned, regally. "Of course she's a princess. She's my granddaughter."

"Come on, I want to see, too," said Ellie. But his arm restrained her.

"In a moment, love. You don't mind if I call you love, now, do you?"

Ellie shook her head, barely able to talk for the happiness that swelled within her.

"Before we see what my mother has up her sleeve for

Princess Amy, you have your first duty as Lady Rothbury
to perform."

"Oh, yes, of course," said Ellie, suddenly apprehensive.
"What must I do?"

He tugged her half a dozen steps to the left and then
stopped. And waited.

"What is it?"

His eyes drifted upwards. Her gaze followed. A branch
twisted with mistletoe.

"Ohh," whispered Ellie. "A kissing bough. That duty I
can see is going to be very arduous. I might need help."
And, standing on tiptoe, she reached up and pulled his
mouth down to hers.

After a moment, they separated reluctantly. "You have
a choice, my love—we go into the drawing room, or
straight up to the bedroom."

Breathlessly, Ellie straightened her gown. "I think it
had better be the drawing room. And then…" she looked
at his mouth and pressed a quick, hungry kiss on it
"…the bedroom."

Arms around each other they strolled towards the
drawing room, pausing every few paces for a kiss. At the
threshold they stopped. Lady Rothbury sat on a small
footstool beside a low table. Amy stood beside her, her
little face a study. Ellie gasped.

Amy turned. Her eyes were shimmering with wonder.
"Look, Mama," she whispered. "Have you ever, ever, *ever,*
seen such a beautiful dolls' house?"

Ellie speechless, shook her head, smiling as the tears
spilled down her cheeks.

"Look, Mr. Bruin."

"You can call me Papa, if you like, Princess." Daniel

turned Ellie in his arms and began to dry her tears. "I thought you told me you weren't a watering pot," he grumbled softly, making her laugh, even as she wept.

"Can I, Mama? Can I call Mr. Bruin Papa?"

"Yes, darling. Of course you can. He is your papa now."

"Good," said the little girl in satisfaction. "I told you that my Christmas wishing candle was special, Mama. It did bring Papa to us."

"Yes darling, it did."

"Look, everyone," said Lady Rothbury suddenly. "It's snowing."

Outside the long windows, across the bright, dancing flames of the red Christmas candles, it began to snow, softly, gently, blanketing the world with white, making everything clean and new and fresh again.

And so it was Christmas Eve. Filled with peace, love, and the promise of joy to come.

There are 24 timeless classics in the Mills & Boon® 100th Birthday Collection

Two of these beautiful stories are out each month. Make sure you collect them all!

If you have missed any of these books, log on to www.millsandboon.co.uk to order your copies online.